Silent Angel

SAMANTHA MICHAELS

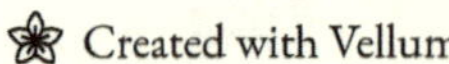
Created with Vellum

Thank you to my husband and our dog for putting up with me! Thank you to my friends and family for their support. Thanks to the other authors I've connected with for being such an inspiration, especially my Weekend Writing Group friends, Lala & JJ. Thank you to my awesome PA Zoe for all her support. Special thanks to the readers for supporting my books!! You're why I keep doing this!!

Prologue

Standing on the side of the road on a bridge overlooking the Susquehanna River, Johnny buried his head in his hands.

"I can't take this fucking loneliness anymore," he said to nobody.

The love of his life was gone, his bandmates were gone, his parents were gone. He was truly alone. Even his angel had stopped coming to visit. He was done ever giving his heart to another. He knew it was going to hurt, but it would be nothing compared to the pain he'd already endured. He had always loved coming here with his dad. They would take his little fishing boat and spend the whole day together. His mom would always wait patiently on the shore, her nose in a book. He started to think about what brought him here.

"Mr. and Mrs Davidson, please come in and have a seat," Dr. Stephens said.

Johnny could tell by the look on his face they were about to get bad news. Katie kept her eyes on Johnny so she didn't notice. Johnny covered her hand with his, squeezing gently.

"I have the results of your latest tests. Tell me when you're ready to hear them."

Johnny looked over at his beloved wife, who just nodded.

"We're ready, Doctor."

"I'm sorry to have to tell you this, but Mrs Davidson's cancer has spread. We're past the point of chemo or surgery."

"What does that mean?" Johnny asked.

"All we can do now is make your wife comfortable. I've asked our hospice nurse to come in to discuss your options."

Katie's face crumpled, and she slumped forward, burying her face in her hands. Johnny watched while her entire body was shaking as she sobbed. Johnny felt his eyes fill with tears, but he willed them away. He knew he had to stay strong for Katie. She would need him now more than ever.

"Shall I ask the nurse to come in?" Dr Stephens asked.

"Please," Johnny said.

Dr Stephens opened the door and returned a few minutes later with the hospital's hospice nurse, Joanne.

"First, let me tell you both how sorry I am," Joanne said. "I'm going to go over your options and your wishes so we can determine the best plan for your situation."

Johnny felt numb as he listened. Once she finished covering everything on her list, she asked Katie for her wishes. Still unable to speak, she pointed toward Johnny.

"We would like to keep Katie at home. We're prepared to do what it takes."

"Very well. I'll schedule an in-home visit for next week, if that's okay. The purpose of the visit will be to assess what equipment you'll need so we can honor Katie's wishes. Just a moment and I'll get you an appointment card."

"Thank you."

After they finished, Katie asked Johnny to call his parents and have them meet at her parents's house.

"Are you sure you're up for that today?"

"I want to get it over with," she said.

Johnny nodded and dialed their number. His mom answered.

"Mom, I need a favor."

"Anything, son."

"Can you and Dad please go to Katie's parents's house?"

"Why?"

Fighting back tears, Johnny said, “We’ll explain when we get there. Please.”

Her voice breaking, she said, “We’re on our way.”

Johnny pulled up in front of his in-laws’s house. He shut off the car and looked at Katie. She looked so small sitting there, hunched over. His heart was breaking, and he had to push that aside. He needed to stay strong for her. He also knew he was going to have to walk away from music. No way could he go on tour or anything now. He’d have to tell the guys tomorrow, and he just hoped they’d understand.

“Are you sure you want to do this now?”

“Yes, please, I need to do this.”

He got out, walked around to her side of the car, and helped her out. He kept a hold of her as they walked up to the front door. He was about to ask her one more time if she was sure she wanted to do this when he saw her reach up and press the doorbell. No turning back now, he thought. Johnny tried to keep a poker face when her father opened the door. Judging by the looks on everyone’s faces, he wasn’t doing a good job. Johnny and Katie sat down on the loveseat across from the sofa where both sets of parents were sitting. He waited a moment for Katie to speak, but all she did was squeeze his hand.

“I don’t know how to tell all of you this,” Johnny started.

“Then I will,” Katie said.

“Are you sure?” Johnny asked.

“I need to do this. My cancer is terminal. All they can do now is make me comfortable. A hospice nurse will come to our home next week. I need you all there with us.”

Katie stood and walked over to her parents, who wrapped her in their embrace, all of them with tears streaming down their faces. Johnny stayed stone-faced, but his parents knew better. They walked over and sat on either side of him, hugging him. Like he’d done so many times today, he fought back tears, determined he would never let anyone see him upset.

“It’s okay to cry, son,” his father said.

“I can’t. Katie needs me to be strong.”

“No, she needs you to be there, and she needs you to deal with this. You won’t be able to help her cope otherwise.”

He knew his parents were trying to help, but he also knew the only thing he could do was stay strong. They stayed a little longer until Katie started yawning. He'd noticed she was getting tired much faster than she used to. When they got home, he helped her into bed and closed the door. He called his bandmates and asked them if they would mind coming over. A little while later, the guys were sitting on the back patio so they wouldn't wake Katie.

"Guys, I hate I have to tell you this, but I can't continue in the band. We found out this morning that Katie's cancer is terminal. I just can't leave her right now, and it wouldn't be fair to all of you."

All three of his bandmates took turns hugging him and telling him they understand his decision. They all knew how much Johnny loved Katie. Despite his continued stoneface, inside he was crying and screaming, feeling lost. He couldn't bear to picture life without her by his side, but he had no choice. She was going to leave him, only in mere months.

Soon after her prognosis, they made some plans for things they wanted to do. They didn't get to do many of them, as Katie's health deteriorated more quickly than anyone had expected. She was at the point that she was in so much pain, they had no choice but to keep her on painkillers, causing to her to do little more than sleep. Johnny kept constant vigil, never once letting himself take a break and deal with this. His parents tried to get him to open up, but he was far too stubborn. Then, one afternoon, it was time. Their assigned hospice nurse, Diane, walked out of the bedroom, tears in her eyes.

She walked over and put her hand on Johnny's arm. "You need to call her family now. It's time for everyone to say their goodbyes."

Johnny nodded and dialed his parents first. They offered to call Katie's parents. Johnny accepted so he could say his goodbyes before anyone else arrived. He walked into the room while Diane waited in the living room to give him privacy. He sat down in the chair next to her bed and took her hand.

"Oh Katie, baby, what am I going to do without you? I love you more than anyone and I'll never stop. I promise you I'll never love another as long as I live."

"No, Johnny, I don't want that. You're too special to be alone. Promise me you'll find your angel."

"I promise," Johnny said.

Johnny sat with her until he heard Diane greet his and Katie's parents, so he walked out.

"I just finished my goodbyes."

Johnny's parents went in first, keeping their time short, so Katie's parents had extra time with their only daughter. When they finished, Diane checked on her. She heard the death rattle start, so she called everyone in. Johnny sat in the chair, while his parents stood behind him, leaving the other two chairs for Katie's parents. Diane stayed near the door, monitoring Katie's vitals on the machines in the corner. She had turned the sound off out of courtesy to the family. When she saw Katie had passed, she walked over and grabbed Johnny's hand to let him know.

Johnny emitted a wail like none his parents had ever heard come out of his mouth. He had lost his one and only love. All his parents could do was hold him, but there was no comforting him. The next several months took a toll on him as he withdrew from everyone. He started having dreams about a woman. She was blonde, wearing a white flowing dress, like an angel. She was always walking in a garden, her back to him. She never spoke or showed her face. Each time he dreamt of her, she was pointing at something different, but always to do with love. He felt like she was trying to tell him to move on and love again, but he just couldn't. The pain he felt when Katie took her last breath was more than he could stand, and he never wanted to experience that again.

Not long after losing their daughter, Katie's parents sold their home and moved to Florida. They couldn't bear living in the same home where they raised Katie, knowing that she would never again come through their front door. Their departure sank Johnny even lower, his last tie to Katie now gone. His parents tried to get him to talk to someone, but he was far too bullheaded for that.

He started fantasizing about her and those fantasies were getting quite steamy. At least this way, he would never get his heart broken, though he missed having a woman in his arms. For now, though, his fantasy woman would have to be enough.

The dreams stopped, sinking Johnny further into a depression until he reached rock bottom. His parents stopped taking no for an answer and made him get help. They had no choice but to lie, telling him they were picking him up to take him out to dinner. Instead, they took him to a support group for grieving spouses. At first, their deceit angered him, but as he attended more and more sessions, he found they were helping. He apologized to his parents for his reaction and thanked them for always being there for him. He knew deep down all they wanted was for him to be happy, and he was grateful. Then they left him too.

It was time. Time to get rid of this pain once and for all. He took a deep breath, trying to calm his nerves. He closed his eyes, taking in the surrounding scents. Fall was coming. You could smell the change in the leaves, feel the crispness in the air. The last season he would ever experience. Suddenly, she appeared. It had been a while, but his angel had returned. She put her hand out to stop him. He sank to his knees and wept, knowing she had just saved his life. He made a promise to her that day and he intended to keep it.

When he got home, he went down to his music and art studio. He needed to capture an image of his angel, so he grabbed a blank canvas and his painting supplies. The next day, Johnny bought a frame to preserve his fantasy woman forever. Little did he know what she still had in store for him...

Chapter One

It was 4 PM on a Friday afternoon in early May. The sun was shining, and the temperatures were warmer than usual for the northern part of Pennsylvania. Johnny Davidson, former kick-ass rock drummer, was heading home from his job as branch manager for a small paper company in Scranton when he heard his cell phone ring. Using the phone button on the steering wheel of his brand new Ford pickup truck, he answered.

"Hello."

"Good afternoon, Mr. Davidson, my name is Jeane Baird, assistant to Patrick Coogan. Mr. Coogan was wondering if you could stop by this afternoon?"

"I'm on my way home from work, so I can swing by. How late will he be there?"

"Mr. Coogan likes to leave by 5 on Fridays."

"I'm only about ten minutes away, so I'll be there shortly."

"Thank you. We'll see you soon."

"Thank you."

As Johnny disconnected, he couldn't help but wonder what his late father's attorney wanted. Anthony Davidson lost his battle with congestive heart failure just this past fall. Just like everyone else Johnny had ever trusted with his heart, his father left him. Not even a wrecking ball could break down the walls he'd built around his heart over the years.

In his twenties, Johnny was a drummer for an up-and-coming hair metal band and married shortly after joining the band. Two years into the marriage, his wife's cancer forced him to abandon his dream and become her caregiver. After she succumbed to her illness, he swore from that moment on, he would never give his heart to another woman. His resolve kept him from that level of pain, but also left him with far too many lonely nights. As he reached his destination, he put the rest of his reverie on hold.

When Johnny walked inside, an older, plump woman with a warm smile greeted him. She reminded him of his beloved grandmother, and he took a liking to her.

"Good afternoon, sir. May I help you?" Jeane asked.

"Yes ma'am. I'm Johnny Davidson. Mr. Coogan is expecting me."

"Of course, we spoke earlier. Right this way, Mr. Davidson.

Jeane rose from her desk and escorted Johnny down the hall to Patrick's office. She knocked and entered when instructed.

"Mr. Davidson is here for his appointment."

"Thank you, Jeane. Please have a seat, Mr. Davidson."

"Johnny is fine."

"Okay, Johnny. I asked you here today as you father left me an envelope that was to be given to you upon his passing."

Patrick opened his drawer and handed the envelope to Johnny.

"Would you like some privacy?"

"No, I'm fine."

Patrick waited while Johnny opened the envelope. Johnny furrowed his brow as he read a small newspaper clipping, then looked at the photo clipped to it.

"Mr. Davidson, is everything okay?"

"I'm not sure," he responded as he handed the clipping to Patrick. "The article is a birth announcement. According to this, I have a twin sister."

"Your father never mentioned having any children other than you. Give me a moment to authenticate this."

A few minutes of typing and the whir of his printer left Johnny with proof that he did indeed have a twin sister.

"Your sister currently lives in Lancaster, PA. I'm unable to provide you with anything more specific without her consent."

"I understand. Thank you for informing me, Mr. Coogan."

"Should you need anything, please call and Jeane will be happy to schedule you an appointment."

Johnny rose and shook Patrick's hand. "Thank you, Mr. Coogan."

"My pleasure. I'll walk you out."

Johnny said an absentminded goodbye to Jeane as he attempted to digest this bombshell. He ran the gamut of emotions, from anger to sadness and landing on hope. After his father's passing, he was alone, with no family to speak of, but all that changed on this fateful afternoon. Johnny didn't know what to do with this information, and spent the weekend in a beer-drunken stupor. After passing out cold on Sunday evening, the alarm awakened him on his cell phone early Monday morning.

As he was getting ready for work, he recalled his dream from the previous night. He was in his car driving down a deserted country road, The Eagles's Hotel California playing as he drove. He didn't know where he was going until he started seeing signs for Lancaster. He encountered a couple of women in his dream, pointing at different signs along his journey. The first was Hannah, as he had looked her up on social media. The second was his fantasy woman. Still the most beautiful blonde woman he'd ever laid eyes on, she pointed at a sign that said LOVE. His silent angel was pointing him toward a new life.

He turned on auto-pilot and arrived to work ahead of his staff. It took him until lunchtime to shake off the fog of his weekend. Thinking clearly for the first time since learning he had a sister, he knew his dream was the answer to his dilemma. Two hours later, his phone rang.

"Johnny Davidson, may I help you?"

"Dave Wilson, corporate VP. I just received your resignation letter. Is there anything I can do to change your mind about leaving us?"

"While I'm grateful for the opportunities I've had here, I have a family matter that needs my attention. I'll be moving to Lancaster once I find housing."

"I understand. If anything changes before your two weeks are up, please let us know. Further, should your circumstances change in the future, you'll always have a place here."

"Thank you, sir."

"Of course. I will ask that you please inform the staff as soon as possible before we interview potential replacements."

"Will do," Johnny said, then disconnected. He contacted his staff via instant message, informing them of a staff meeting at 2 PM. Once the group had gathered in the conference room, he informed them of his resignation, citing personal reasons, and letting them know they were welcome to apply if so inclined.

Johnny found a rental house rather quickly, as new homes had just been built and not yet occupied. They approved his application. He contacted his real estate agent, who assured him she would handle the sale of his home, allowing him to move to Lancaster the first week of June.

Johnny's last day was a celebration. He was a well-respected manager and his staff was sorry to see him go. After walking out the front door one last time, he headed home and packed up a couple week's worth of clothes and other items, planning to leave for his new home first thing Saturday morning. He put on one of his favorite bands, Alex Rudi Pell. His favorite song, Eternal Prisoner, came on. As he listened to the words, he couldn't help but wonder if he'd ever stop being a prisoner of his grief. He wanted to have a woman in his arms again, but that demon just wouldn't let his heart be free.

What was a two hour drive took him closer to four because of tourists. Lancaster was one of Pennsylvania's more popular travel destinations, especially during warmer weather. Thankful that he left bright and early, he made it to the leasing office before closing to sign the lease and get the keys to his new home. Before returning to his car, he asked the leasing manager if he knew his sister.

"Yes, as a matter of fact I do. She owns and operates a successful pet supply store here in town. I'm afraid I can't say much more, but as the name is public knowledge, I can tell you her store is called Rock the Fur."

"Thank you so much, sir."

"Of course. Best wishes in your new home. I hope it brings you joy and happy memories."

Johnny nodded and walked out, knowing full well that there would be no happy memories. While he longed for a special woman to share his life with, he could never allow himself the risk of another devastating heartbreak. He punched his new address into his GPS and continued his life's brand new journey.

After carrying his stuff inside, he sat down on the couch and started thinking about the tragedy that changed his life forever, leaving him unable to trust another with his heart, and unable to pull himself out of his constant feeling of despair. He couldn't believe it was twenty years ago that he lost Katie.

Chapter Two

Eden Mitchell, owner of Garden of Eden, was finishing her nightly cleaning. Garden of Eden was one of the up-and-coming restaurants in town, attracting residents and tourists in droves. She was proud of her success, especially given the circumstances that led her here. Sometimes, though, she couldn't shake the incredible feeling of loneliness that filled her heart. As Eden drove home, she couldn't help but think about her fantasy man.

Eden had always been a huge rock fan, her fantasies always filled with a sexy musician or ten. Her fantasies got even stronger when she married her dud of an ex-husband. She imagined a tall, muscular man with broad shoulders and a sexy chest. She didn't know why, but she always saw the phrase veni, vidi, vici when she thought of him. At least with this one, I don't have to worry about having my heart broken; she thought to herself. She knew she could never give her heart to another man after what her ex-husband had put her through. The betrayal by him and her family would have taken most people down. Eden somehow found the strength to overcome it.

Once she arrived home and went inside, she sat down on her couch. Her mind took her back to the lowest point in her life. She was in her junior year at the University of Penn when she met Todd. They had both come from wealthy families, neither of whom had any trouble paying for the high tuition of the Ivy League. She liked Todd, but he inspired nothing more than friendship in her. Their families, however, were more than delighted at their pairing, and for the first time in her life, her parents approved of something she did. At their joint graduation party, Todd proposed to Eden, which she accepted to maintain their approval. They were married at the ritziest wedding venue in Philadelphia before departing on a month-long honeymoon to Hawaii.

Todd earned his law degree and, after their honeymoon, took and passed the bar, then joined his father's firm. Eden's degree was a BA in English. From the time she was a small child, she loved books. It had always been her dream to be a writer. Her favorite books were romance novels. The steamier the better. Her favorite stories to write always involved bad boy rock stars. Her family couldn't have been more disappointed that she didn't follow her parents into business.

Despite graduating Magna Cum Laude, her parents still saw her as a failure, unlike her perfect older sister, Morgan the Magnificent, Eden's less-than-flattering secret nickname for her. Morgan was also attending Penn, but chose the Wharton School of Business. Despite not earning the level of academic accolades Eden had, her parents couldn't have been prouder. In fact, the only thing that redeemed Eden in their eyes was her marriage to Todd. Todd earned a large six-figure salary, so he expected Eden to be a housewife, which she loathed. Her only saving grace was having a lot of time on her hands to write.

Todd was attractive and had a large bank account, but he was a dud, especially in bed. Eden always went through the motions, but there was no spark, no passion. Todd was often away on business trips or lengthy court cases, so Eden would imagine being a rockstar's wife. She spent a lot of time on social media, ogling her favorite musicians. Still, she stayed with Todd because that was what her family expected of her. So many times she thought about running away, but would just let herself get lost in her stories.

About two years into their marriage, Todd started talking about having children. Eden had never wanted children, but again, she knew he expected her to, so she stopped her birth control. After a year of not conceiving, Todd demanded she see a fertility doctor. After a battery of tests, the doctor determined she couldn't conceive. Instead of comforting her, Todd blew up, screaming at her right in front of her doctor before storming out. That moment began the end of their marriage. Todd started spending more and more late nights "at the office."

To make matters worse, instead of supporting her, not just Todd's family but also her own family, blamed her for not giving them grandchildren. It didn't matter that it was out of Eden's hands. They resented her. They never tried to hide that resentment and even when she caught Todd red-handed having an affair with Morgan, they still sided with him. Despite everything, Eden stayed, pretending to be the happy little housewife.

One afternoon, about a year ago, Eden was sitting on their patio, laptop open, writing another steamy rockstar romance and listening to her favorite hair metal bands when the lyrics of one of her favorite songs awakened something inside her. As loud as she could, she sang along with Dee Snider, telling anyone in earshot that she'd reached the end of her rope. She closed her laptop, carried it upstairs and packed. After loading her car, she took off, not stopping until she reached Lancaster, her favorite place to visit.

She checked into a hotel until she could find permanent housing. The next morning, she found a lawyer and filed for divorce. In order to keep his family's good name intact, her ex-father-in-law paid her a handsome settlement for never speaking of the affair to any members of the press. Using part of her settlement, she opened Garden of Eden, then bought herself a modest home, dividing the rest between a savings account and a variety of investments. Sometimes she wondered if it was time to think about dating again, but after what Todd put her through, she didn't know if she'd ever be ready. At least her fantasy man wouldn't object to the dirty words she liked to use in bed.

All that reminiscing left her feeling wiped out, so after spending a little time on her laptop writing and checking out the latest trends on social media, she headed off to bed, as she needed to be up early to open the restaurant. She laid there wondering what it would feel like to be wrapped in her fantasy man's arms as she drifted off to sleep.

When she arrived the following morning, she saw Hannah and Mikael, so she waved. Every time she saw them, they were holding hands or touching. She was happy they found each other, but a small part of her felt jealous that she didn't have someone. No time to dwell on that now, as the breakfast rush would start soon and she needed to make sure she had plenty of coffee ready. Once all the pots were brewing, she sat down up front and did a little more writing while she waited for the coffee to finish. About five minutes after she opened, she had a crowd and almost couldn't keep up. Once the breakfast rush died down, she had some time to relax.

She was reading over some of the recent stories she'd written about her fantasy man. She looked up for a minute and swore she saw him outside. She looked away then returned her gaze to the window, but nobody was there. Great, she thought, now I'm hallucinating. She decided she needed to take the rest of the day off, so she went to the kitchen to make sure Max would be okay with just the night manager if she could come in. Max agreed, so once the night manager arrived, Eden headed home. She spent some time reading, writing, and watching TV, then headed to bed.

She woke up in the morning feeling refreshed, grateful that it was the weekend. She went to the park. She loved sitting on the dock by the lake and always found peace there, watching the water ripple, listening to the birds, and just being by herself. She had gotten used to being her own company. Sometimes, though, she craved the touch of another, but she could always push that away. She heard footsteps approaching and when she turned to look, she swore she saw her fantasy man again. She was so rattled that she left the park.

Chapter Three

The next morning, Johnny was feeling restless, so he got in his truck and started driving to get the lay of the land. He was also feeling especially down today. His silent angel hadn't visited his dreams in a while and he missed her. During his travels, he found the local park. He parked his truck, then started walking around the path. As he got to the back of the park, he saw a lake with a small dock. He stopped dead in his tracks. Sitting on the dock was his silent angel. What the hell, he thought, I'm wide awake. How can I be seeing her? He shook his head, and when he looked again, the dock was empty. Johnny chalked it up to needing sleep and continued his walk. When he finished a lap, he sat down on the bench, his mind filled with visions of his fantasy woman.

After a little while, he returned to his truck and searched for Rock the Fur, then drove over. He parked across the street. The store had a large glass window so he could see inside with ease. After a little while, he saw her. He almost got out of his car and went inside, but what would he say?

"Oh hey, I'm your long-lost twin brother?"

He saw a sign on the door that they were looking for a manager, so he went in and applied.

"Can I help you?" the man whose name tag read Kurt asked.

"I'd like to apply for the manager's position."

"Great, one moment please."

Kurt handed him an application and walked him to a small table so he could fill it out. He listed his name using his old stage name, Johnny Thunder. Once he was done, he handed it back to Kurt.

"Thank you. The owners are on their honeymoon, so they'll be in touch when they return."

"Wonderful, thank you so much."

When he walked outside and looked across the street, he saw a restaurant called Garden of Eden, sending chills down his spine. He started thinking of his fantasy woman, his Silent Angel. He'd chosen that name for her after hearing another song by Axel. One line in the song references the garden of Eden. That left him wondering if the restaurant was some sort of omen for him. Just as he was about to go inside, he got a strange feeling and changed his mind. He stopped for takeout on the way, unable to shake whatever changed his mind about entering the restaurant.

Johnny spent the next several weeks working on unpacking and setting up his new home, while waiting to hear about the job. One Friday afternoon, his phone rang, and he saw the name of Hannah's shop on his caller ID.

"Hello."

"Mr. Thunder, this is Mikael Alfredsson. I'm calling about the job you applied for. Are you available today to come in and talk?"

"Sure. What time?"

"Will an hour from now work?"

"Yes, thank you."

"See you then."

After he disconnected, he grabbed a shower and threw on a polo shirt and a pair of khakis, then headed down. Kurt greeted him and walked him back to the office, where Mikael was waiting. He didn't see Hannah anywhere, but he didn't want to ask or Mikael might get suspicious. Mikael stood and extended his hand, and Johnny returned the gesture.

"Please have a seat," Mikael requested.

Johnny sat in the chair across from the desk and said, "Thank you."

"I should thank you for making this so easy."

"How so?"

"You're work history and experience are just what we need, so I'd like to skip the formalities and offer you the position. My wife agreed when I showed her the application. If you're still interested, we can go over salary and benefits."

"I am. Thank you so much for this opportunity."

They spent the next hour going over all the information and filling out all the paperwork.

"Is a week from Monday too soon for you to start?"

"Not at all."

"Great. Both stores are busy and we could use the help."

Mikael stood, so Johnny followed suit. He walked Johnny out and told him he'd see him in about a week. After working on the house all day, he was starving, so he made himself a sandwich then took a walk around his neighborhood, hoping to clear his mind. It had been a whirlwind, and he was feeling overwhelmed. The walk did little to help, so when he got back home, he went down to the basement and sat behind his drum kit. He spent the next hour playing and was finally feeling calm.

Music always made him the happiest, especially sharing it with a beautiful woman. Like he had many times before, he wished he could bring his dream woman to life. He sighed, knowing that could never happen, and besides, he would be too afraid to lose her like he'd lost everyone else. He headed up to bed, enjoying a visit from his beautiful angel while he slept.

Johnny's first day of work had arrived and Mikael wasn't kidding that they were swamped. Mikael gave him a quick lesson on using their computer system, then left to take care of customers. Getting the chance to talk with people about music was natural for Johnny, so he impressed his new boss. He couldn't help but wonder how Mikael would feel about him once he told Hannah who he was. No time to worry about that now, given the traffic in and out of the store. The next couple of weeks were the same, so Johnny didn't have time to focus on anything but the job.

One Friday afternoon, things were slower, so Hannah let Kurt have an early start to his weekend. Mikael was also away from the shop, helping his friend Dean with something, so Johnny found himself alone with Hannah. He knew he was going to have to drop the bombshell on her soon, so might as well be now. He saw Hannah heading his way, and his nerves kicked in, but he was determined not to chicken out.

"Hey there. I realized we haven't had much of a chance to talk and get to know each other," she said.

"I've wanted to, but it's been busy. That's so great that you've built something so successful."

"Thank you. If I may ask, what brought you to Lancaster?"

"I had some family issues to tend to, so here I am."

"Have you lived here before? Since the first time I saw you, something felt familiar about you."

"I did for a short time as a young child, but I have no actual memories, just pictures."

"If I'm not prying, what was it that made you move here?"

"I came to town after my father passed away. His death left me with no family, at least until his lawyer gave me an envelope upon my dad's death."

"I'm so sorry. I understand. My father also passed away."

"I'm so sorry."

"Thank you. So, this letter said you actually have family?"

"Yes, so I came to town to find her."

"Wow. What's her name? I may know her or be able to help?"

"Thank you for the offer, but I've found her."

"Wow, how exciting. What was meeting her like?"

"You tell me," he said.

"What do you mean?"

"I'm your twin brother."

"I don't understand. I'm an only child. My dad left my mom when I was very young. My mom and step-father raised me."

"My father and the woman I thought was my mother raised me. I didn't find out until after my father, our father, passed that she was my step-mom."

Tears spilled out of Hannah's eyes. "Why are you telling me these lies?"

"I promise you, I'm telling the truth." He handed her the envelope his dad's lawyer had given him.

Hannah removed the contents and laid them out on the counter. After reading the birth announcement, she looked up at Johnny, fresh tears in her eyes. He braced himself for her to yell at him or throw him out. Instead, much to his surprise, she threw her arms around his neck. He returned her embrace, his own eyes also filling with tears.

"I have so much I want to talk about, but please understand, I'm going to need some time to process this."

"Of course. I thought you were going to react differently, so I'm grateful you didn't throw me out."

Before Johnny could respond, they saw Mikael approaching them, looking puzzled.

"Is everything okay?" Mikael asked.

"You won't believe this, but come look," Hannah said.

Johnny stayed silent, letting Mikael finish looking at everything that was in his envelope.

"I don't think I could ever have guessed this in a million years," Mikael said.

"Me either," Hannah said.

Looking at Johnny, Mikael said, "How long have you known?"

"I only found out right before I moved down here. I was called to my, I mean, our father's lawyer's office. He gave me the envelope, and I was just as shocked by its contents. I grew up thinking the woman who raised me was my biological mother. There was never any mention of the divorce, of having a sister, or anything else."

"There's so much I want to ask you about," Hannah said, "but I need some time to deal with this first," she repeated.

"I understand. I'll collect my things," Johnny said.

"What do you mean? You're not quitting, are you?" Hannah asked.

"I thought you would ask me to leave after this."

"Not at all. I want you here and I do want to get to know you."

"Thank you."

They worked in silence for the rest of the afternoon, other than talking with customers. It was awkward, but had still gone better than Johnny had expected. He had a lot he wanted to talk to her about, especially what their mom was like. He didn't even know if she was still alive. If she was, would she want to see him? There was so much running through his head, he was having a hard time staying focused. He was relieved when it was time to head home for the day.

Chapter Four

When his shift was done, Johnny headed over to Garden of Eden for dinner. He'd been wanting to try seeing what that strange feeling was about, but his mind had been preoccupied with Hannah.

He walked inside and waited to be seated. His jaw dropped when he saw her come out of the kitchen. Her long blonde hair was in a loose braid. Jeans and a Led Zeppelin t-shirt replaced the white flowing gown, but he knew it was her. No wonder I had such a strange feeling, he thought to himself. She greeted him with a warm smile, and his heart melted.

She stopped dead in her tracks when she walked out to the counter. The man standing there waiting for a table reminded her of her fantasy man and her heart started racing. Was she losing her mind this time? She knew she needed to walk up front, but her feet couldn't remember how to move. After a few minutes of standing there, she composed herself and walked up to the counter.

"Good Evening."

"Hello."

"How many are in your party?"

"Just me."

"Right this way."

Eden walked him to an empty table in the corner and handed him a menu. She took his drink order, then left him to peruse his options. A few minutes later, she returned with his iced tea.

"Have you decided, sir?"

"It's Johnny, and yes. I would like to try the chicken sandwich on rye bread."

"Coming right up, Johnny."

"Thank you."

He watched Eden smile and head to the kitchen to give her cook the order. His eyes scanned the restaurant. He noticed her picture on the wall, telling patrons she was the owner, Eden Mitchell. Her loose-fitting clothes caressed her curves just right. Johnny felt his mouth water. Stop it, he chastised himself. You know what will happen if you get involved, and this woman is far too beautiful to be taken from this earth. More than anything, he wanted to find someone who would stay in his life forever, but if his past taught him anything, that wasn't in the cards for him. He fought back tears as images of his beloved wife consumed his thoughts, lying in a hospital bed in their home, a shell of her former self. All the tubes and machines, the steady presence of their nurse, along with family and friends, was too much to handle, and he never wanted to be in that place again.

A few minutes later, Eden brought him dinner.

"If you need anything, give me a shout."

"Thank you."

His sandwich was delicious, but not as delicious as she was. When he finished eating, he walked up front to pay his bill.

"My compliments to your chef. The sandwich was great," he complimented.

"I'll tell him."

"Thank you. Have a wonderful evening."

"You as well."

He smiled, then walked out the door and headed home.

The next day, he took his lunch hour at Eden's restaurant, because of her delicious food, but also to avoid being alone with Hannah. She had said little to him since learning who he was. He hoped that would change, but he understood that she needed time, so he didn't push her. Eden was standing up front when he walked inside.

"Nice to see you again, Johnny."

"I was so impressed the last time I was here, I came back."

With a warm smile, she said, "Follow me," and walked him to his table. After handing him a menu, she excused herself, giving him time to decide what he wanted. One look at her and he knew. He also knew it could never happen. Perhaps they could become friends, and even that was risky. She returned a few minutes later and took his order. He ordered a chicken salad sandwich and a side of potato salad, along with an iced tea. As no cooking was required, he was eating after only a few minutes.

When he finished eating, he walked up front to pay his check. The minute Eden came to the register to help him, his breath caught in his throat as his heart started racing. He talked himself down, but made a note to avoid this establishment for future dining needs. He couldn't allow himself to get involved, and he knew from the moment he saw her that resisting her would be impossible. He complimented her establishment, then headed out the door.

After arriving home, he downed a couple of beers then headed to his new basement to pound on his drums. Drumming was a stress-reliever, but not today. He gave up and went for a walk around his new neighborhood, returning home about an hour later. After a few hours of watching TV, he headed to bed, exhausted from his eventful day. A certain blonde in a flowing white dress filled his dreams, causing him to wake up drenched in sweat.

Despite his plan to avoid her restaurant, Johnny couldn't stay away and started spending every day at Garden of Eden. He loved how she treated her customers, but he wanted to be more than just that. He could use a friend. She was one of the most stunning women he'd ever seen. She was a woman of few words, but her angelic smile more than made up for it. My silent angel, he thought to himself. Maybe she would be the one who would never leave. Again, he had to yell at himself to stop these thoughts, knowing the reality that it would only end in heartbreak.

Wanting more than anything to talk to her, he returned near closing time one night. He asked for a table in the back corner and stayed until the last customer had left.

"Can I get you anything else?"

"The pleasure of your company."

"I'm flattered, but I couldn't."

"Why not? I won't bite. I mean, unless you want me to."

For the first time in the short time he'd been coming here, Eden laughed. Even her laugh was angelic, he thought, his dick stirring. Down boy, he told himself.

"You have a beautiful laugh. You should do that more."

"If only I had reason to. I guess it wouldn't hurt to take a quick break."

Johnny stood and pulled her chair out for her, then pushed it in once she sat.

"Wow, there are still a few gentlemen left."

"Can I get you something to eat and drink?"

"That's my job."

"Nonsense. You spend all day taking care of others. Let me return the favor."

"I couldn't."

"I insist. What would you like?"

"A chicken salad sandwich and water sounds perfect, but you don't have to."

"I know."

"Thank you."

"My pleasure."

Johnny returned with her order, as well as another iced tea for himself.

"Have you always lived in Lancaster?" she asked.

"No. I needed a change of scenery, so I moved down here."

"Where did you live before?"

"Scranton."

"Not too much of a change, then."

"It's a bit more rural than the part of town I lived in, and a welcome change."

"I love it here. I moved from Philadelphia, so I understand it being a welcome change."

"How long have you been here?"

"About a year, but I've only owned the restaurant a few months."

"I haven't eaten anywhere else, but so far, this is my favorite!"

"Thank you, but I'm not on the market."

"I beg your pardon."

"I'm not interested in dating right now."

"I hope I didn't give you that impression. I don't know anyone in town, and was just attempting to make a friend."

"I'm sorry. I get some weirdos that come in and a woman has to keep her guard up."

"I understand. I would love if we could be friends, nothing more."

"I suppose that would be nice. I don't have many of those."

"Then it's settled."

After Eden finished eating, Johnny stayed and helped her clean up, then walked her to her car, as it was dark. She thanked him and smiled before driving off. Johnny waved as she drove away, then got in his truck and headed home. The minute her car was out of sight, he missed her. He went home and headed to bed. As he laid there waiting to fall asleep, he couldn't help but imagine what Eden would feel like in his arms. He pushed that thought out of his head and fell asleep. He got up early the next morning so he could grab breakfast before work.

Johnny walked in and saw a long line of customers. so he walked behind the counter and started helping pour coffee while she took food orders. With his help, she could get her busy clientele in and out with speed. Once the morning rush slowed, she sat down for a rest and Johnny joined her.

"Sorry I couldn't say this sooner, but good morning," she said.

"Good morning to you."

Damn, he was sexy, she thought to herself. She couldn't help but gawk at his handsome face and muscular physique. Warm from helping her, he removed his jacket, revealing forearms covered with beautiful artwork. She found it impossible to resist a sexy man with tattoos. She couldn't help but notice Johnny was having one hell of an effect on her.

"I hope this isn't too personal, but were you ever in a band?" she asked.

"How could you tell?"

"You give off that brooding rock star vibe. Let me guess, you were a drummer?"

"Wow, I'm impressed. Ever since I was a small child, I beat on anything I could get my hands on. Wooden spoons on pots was my favorite until my parents gave in and told Santa to bring me a drum kit for Christmas."

"That's so awesome."

"I never took one lesson. Instead, I learned by listening. John Bonham and Neil Peart were my biggest inspirations. I joined a hair metal band while still in high school, but the timing wasn't right, so I had to put my sticks away and enter the workforce. I never lost my passion for it, though, and I have a full drum kit in my basement."

"I'd love to come hear you play some time. Much to the dismay of my uptight family, I've been a rock fan my entire life."

"That's the first time you mentioned your family. Tell me about them, if you want."

"I'd love to, but not here. I try to keep my personal life away from work."

"I understand. Maybe we could have dinner one night, unless you work late every night?"

"No, it was just last night that my night manager was off. As long as you promise this is just two friends sharing a meal and not a date, it would be nice to not eat alone for once."

"I've been told I make a mean taco, so I'd love to cook for us."

"Now you're talking. I love tacos."

"How does tonight sound?"

"I don't have any plans, not that I do any other night either, so tonight would be fine."

"Great," he said as he grabbed a piece of paper and wrote his address down. "Does 6 o'clock work?"

"I'll be there."

"In that case, I need to head to the store to grab some things. I'll see you later."

"Looking forward to it."

Johnny's hand brushed hers when he handed her the paper with his address, sending quite the sensation through her body. What the hell was that? Johnny waved as he walked out. Eden didn't have time to think about what happened as a few minutes later, her lunch rush started, so her focus turned to her customers. Once the afternoon lull hit, she sat down and her thoughts returned to what had happened earlier.

She couldn't believe she had agreed to have dinner with Johnny, even if it was just as friends. It had been so long since she'd been in the company of a man, she wasn't sure how to behave. Johnny was different, though. He couldn't have been any more opposite the stuffed shirts she had to pretend she enjoyed keeping company with. She left work around 4:30, stopped at the liquor store to grab a bottle of wine to bring with her, then went home to shower and change. A little before 6, she knocked on Johnny's door. The door opened and Eden almost passed out. Johnny opened the door and Eden was staring at the sexiest man she'd ever laid eyes on, dressed in black leather pants and a black silk shirt with a couple of buttons open.

"Hi, Eden, please come in."

Rendered speechless, she handed him the wine, then attempted to figure out how to make her legs work. Johnny chuckled at her reaction, as she could regain her composure and speak.

"You look great," Eden said.

"As do you. Thank you for the wine."

"You're welcome."

"Please have a seat. Dinner's almost ready."

"Can I help?"

"Absolutely not, you're my guest."

She smiled and sat down. A few minutes later, Johnny carried everything over to the table. He had everything in bowls so they could build their tacos the way they wanted them. He also grabbed two wine glasses and poured them each a glass of Moscato from the bottle Eden brought. After they finished eating, Eden insisted on helping clean up. When they were done, she had a special request for Johnny.

"Could I go see your drum kit and maybe hear a song?"

"I'd be honored."

They walked down to the basement. Eden was star-struck at all the rock memorabilia he had all over the room. For the first time since her youth, Eden felt alive. Johnny grabbed a pair of sticks and sat down on the stool behind the drums.

"Any requests?"

"I'd love to hear one of my all-time favorites. Can you play Paint it Black?"

". Hope you enjoy."

Johnny started playing as Eden sang the words in her head. He was talented and she couldn't believe he never made it big. By the time he was done, she felt like she was at a concert, and before she realized it, she was head-banging and throwing up the horns. When he was done, Johnny stood and took a bow.

"That was incredible. Thank you so much."

"My pleasure."

They headed back upstairs and sat down on his couch.

"I'm curious about something," Johnny said.

"What's that?"

"The first day I came into your restaurant, you looked you'd seen a ghost."

"In a manner of speaking, yes. I've been having dream and fantasies about a man I created. You remind me of him, so when I saw you, I thought I was losing my mind. I couldn't help but notice your shocked expression when you saw me. What was that about?"

"You aren't the only one who was having dreams. I've been having them for years. She even led me here after I found out about Hannah. Just like you, she reminded me of the woman I call my silent angel."

"I don't know what to say. I've always been a big believer in fate and it sure seems like it brought us together."

"It does. My turn for a question. When I asked you earlier about your family, you seemed a little unsure you wanted to tell me anything."

"I was, but while it would do me some good to talk about it, I'm always hesitant."

"Why?"

"I had a tough upbringing, but when people find out my family was wealthy, they belittle what I went through."

"I promise I won't judge."

Eden took a deep breath and said, "Here goes."

Chapter Five

"My parents both came from money. My dad came from a line of wealthy businessmen, as did my mom. My father, Brighton, is the owner and CEO of a consulting company. I always felt their marriage was more of a business arrangement than anything else. They expected their offspring to be the same way. My older sister was exactly that. Then along came Eden. I had zero interest in business. I was a dreamer, a silly heart, as they called me. I loved books and music. They were ashamed of me, especially my mother, Priscilla, so they didn't invite me downstairs when they had their snooty parties. I took that time alone, and believe me, it was a lot of time, and made up stories."

"What type of stories?" Johnny asked.

"As a child, it was fantasies about being in a family that loved me. As I got into my teenage years, it was being whisked away by the rock stars I loved listening to. The common theme throughout was getting away from my family."

"I'm sorry they put you through that."

"Thanks. I wish that was where the story ended, but I understand if you're tired of hearing me talk."

"Not at all."

Eden took another deep breath.

"I thought college would be my saving grace."

"And it wasn't?"

"My parents set up a trust for my sister and I that became ours upon our eighteenth birthday to pay for college. They were livid when I declared English not business as my major, but they couldn't take the money back. So off to Penn I went."

"Impressive. I love a woman with a brain."

Eden blushed at his compliment.

"In my junior year, I met Todd. I later found out that was setup by our families, an attempt by my parents to reign me in and it worked for a while. He was charming enough, but he was a total dud in the sack."

Johnny laughed.

"Poor guy, couldn't have been that bad."

"Wanna bet? The first time I tried dirty talk in bed, his dick went limp. He forbade me ever to use that language again."

"What the fuck? There're dudes out there that don't like that? I can say that's a first. Must be the questionable company I keep," he quipped.

"Our marriage was the same as growing up with my family. This broke my spirit, other than sneaking in some very steamy writing and reading when he was at work."

"That's my kinda woman."

Eden felt a warmth between her legs, but pushed it aside and kept talking.

"One afternoon, I had enough, so I packed up my shit and left. I did just fine in the divorce as they didn't want their precious name dragged through the mud, given Todd was fucking my bitch of a sister. Then, about six months after I left, I see an article in the newspaper that they were married in a private ceremony."

"Damn, sounds like something out of a movie."

Eden laughed and Johnny felt his dick stir.

"So here I am, ostracized by my family and alone."

"Wrong, you're not alone. You have me."

"Thanks. You've been a great friend so far. I didn't realize how lonely I was until you came into my restaurant and made me sit with you."

"Trust me, I needed a friend as much as you did."

"I've never felt this comfortable with anyone. I've never told another soul the things I've told you tonight."

"I'm honored."

"So, you've heard me ramble for far too long. Now it's your turn."

"I think we need to save that for another time."

Eden looked at her watch, shocked that it was almost eleven. "You're right. If I don't get to bed soon, I'll be useless in the morning."

She stood to get ready to go. Johnny walked her to her car. Before she got in, she gave him a hug, sending a warming sensation throughout his body.

"Thank you for dinner and for listening to me."

"My pleasure. Let's get together this weekend, and I'll give you some insight into the wonder that is Johnny."

"I'm intrigued. Talk to you soon."

"You can count on it."

She got in her car and waved as she backed out of his driveway. Johnny stood outside until he could no longer see her car. He sat down on the porch for a few minutes, his thoughts consumed by the beautiful angel that just left. She made it clear that she only wanted to be friends, but he was feeling something more for her. I'll have to put that aside, he thought to himself. Having her as a friend was better than not having her at all.

Johnny continued being a daily visitor at her restaurant during his lunch breaks. Hanging out with Eden was his favorite pastime. He stopped in on Friday morning to firm up their plans for Saturday, then he headed across the street to work. When his shift was done, he walked back across to her restaurant.

"Mind if I hang out until you're done?"

"Have a seat. I don't have a night manager tonight, so I'm closing."

"Okay, put me to work, then."

"Don't be silly, you didn't come here for that."

"I want to."

"Okay, thank you."

Once the last few customers left, Eden locked the door and turned off her open sign. She started wiping down tables. Johnny followed her, lifting the chairs onto each table so she didn't have to. Once that was done, she wiped down the counter while Johnny grabbed her mop and cleaned the floor. She had to admit, it was nice having some help. Add to that, watching Johnny's muscles as he worked was nothing to complain about. Once everything was done, Eden turned out all the lights, then walked out to the parking lot. Johnny waited until she was in her car, then he went home. He couldn't wait to see her tomorrow, as he was enjoying getting to know her.

Saturday rolled around and he was sitting and watching some TV when he heard his door, smiling when he saw Eden.

"Would you object to a small change in plans?" Johnny asked.

"What'd you have in mind?" Eden said, trying to quell the naughty thoughts invading her head.

"Most of my clothes are suits or casual, so I need more 'in between' clothes for work and I hate shopping."

"You're in luck. I took care of all the shopping for my ex, so I'm an expert at picking out men's clothes. Let's go."

She drove Johnny to Tanger Outlets and parked in front of the Brooks Brothers outlet. After only about an hour, Johnny had at least two weeks' worth of stuff.

"Thank you so much for helping me."

"Of course. Now, how about dinner?"

"Do you like Chinese food?"

"One of my favorites. I know the perfect place. Do you know what you want?"

She told Johnny what she wanted and once he decided what he was hungry for, he called the order in since she was driving. After they grabbed the food, they went back to Johnny's house and enjoyed dinner together, then retired to his living room.

"Okay, you promised I would get to hear about your childhood," she said.

"I was hoping you'd forget."

"If you're not comfortable talking about it, I understand."

"Not at all. Just not always comfortable talking about myself."

"I get that. Contrary to what you've seen, I'm not either. I feel different around you than pretty much anyone I've ever known."

"I feel the same, so here goes."

"We didn't have the level of wealth as your family, but we were never lacking. My parents were amazing."

"Were?"

"My mom passed away two years ago and my father, a few weeks before I moved here. I'm an only child, so that left me with nobody. I was feeling like a change in scenery was what I needed, but I wasn't sure where. Then, after some information I received, I decided I needed to move here."

"I'm so sorry you had to go through that."

"It was hard, but I should be used to it. Everyone I've ever loved left me. I was married in my late twenties, but the marriage only lasted two years?"

Eden put a hand on Johnny's arm, sending a spark through him.

"If I may, what happened?"

"Cancer. Katie's form was aggressive, and she passed away. Her death devastated me, but I was thankful that she was no longer suffering. And this one I feel guilty about; my former bandmates. They found a replacement for me and booked some gigs to get noticed. Their tour bus was involved in a horrific accident and none of them survived.

Tears in her eyes, all she could say was, "Oh, Johnny, I'm sorry."

"Thanks. I've dated plenty since losing her, but I haven't been able to get serious with anyone."

"Different circumstances, but I get it."

She moved closer and gave him a hug. He returned the gesture, his heart beating out of his chest. The thought that the universe put her into his life for a reason consumed his brain. But was that reason to be friends, or were they destined for something more? No, he scolded himself, it can be nothing more. Eden is far too special to be taken from this world, so he could never let himself get involved with her.

"I really had a great childhood. My parents loved each other, and that always stuck with me, especially when I watched so many of my classmates go through their parents' divorcing. I'm almost hesitant to tell you anymore after what yours put you through."

"Don't be. I love hearing your story. It reminds me of a lot of the things I fantasized about."

"They never tried to discourage me from music. Their only request was that I also apply myself in school, so I earned decent grades, graduated on time, and played music. I could always tell my parents were proud of me and that meant the world to me. They would have been upset to see the way your parents treated you."

"They sound amazing. I wish I could have had the chance to meet them."

"So do I. They would have loved to get to know you. I sure have."

He saw Eden's cheeks redden, a sheepish smile on her face. He knew for sure the effect she was having on him, but was he having one on her too? His mind started wandering, filled with thoughts of what it would be like to hold her, to kiss her, to be naked with her, and he liked all of it. Fuck, he thought, am I falling for this woman? I just can't. His mind was so preoccupied, he didn't even notice Eden talking to him until she raised her voice.

"Earth to Johnny. Where were you?"

"Sorry about that. I get lost in thoughts."

"That's something I get. That's where my story ideas start. I was saying it must be tough no longer having any family," she repeated.

"Here's where it gets interesting. I found out I do. That's why I moved here."

"What do you mean?"

Johnny told her the whole story about Hannah. She just sat there in disbelief.

"Wow. I'm not sure how to respond. How does Hannah feel about it?"

"I showed her the proof, so she believes me, but she and Mikael told me they needed time to sort through it before we talk."

"That sounds like the drama you'd only find in a novel."

"Speaking of novels, I'd love to read some of your writing sometime."

"Nobody's ever asked before."

"Then let me be the first."

"Okay, I'll look at what I have and print something for you to read."

"Can't wait."

He couldn't help but hope it was something naughty. He was interested in knowing what her dirtiest thoughts and fantasies were.

"So, I'm curious. What other stuff do you like to do? I'd love to hang out somewhere other than my house sometime."

"There's a great rock club here in town. I've never gone as it felt weird to go alone, but I've heard they get some awesome local bands playing. Maybe we could do that one night. They have karaoke a few nights a week as well."

"I'd love to."

Eden smiled. She thought about walking into the club with Johnny. What the hell is this guy doing to me? For the first time in far too long, she could see herself in a relationship again. That thought both excited and terrified her, though she had to admit, excitement was winning. Looking at Johnny sitting across from her, remembering their embrace, she longed to feel that again. The whole time he'd been talking, she couldn't take her eyes off his sexy lips and the places she'd love for him to use them. Deep down, she craved that passion and intimacy she never had with Todd. Was Johnny brought into her life to do just that? His voice interrupted her reverie.

"I see I'm not the only one drifting tonight," he said.

"Sorry about that."

"No need. You know I understand."

Feeling nervous after her last thoughts, she said, "I better head out. It's getting late."

"Okay. I had a great time, thank you."

"I did too. I'll talk to you soon," she said.

Johnny again walked her to her car then went back inside when she was out of sight. He wanted nothing more than to beg her to stay. He wanted that woman in his bed more than he'd ever wanted anything or anyone. He was trying hard to fight his feelings for her, but it was becoming a losing battle. Maybe I should stay away for a while, he thought to himself as he drifted off to sleep.

Chapter Six

A couple of weeks had gone by since their last dinner together, and Eden hadn't seen or heard from Johnny. She couldn't help but wonder if she'd done or said something that upset him, and if she had, she would rather have had Johnny tell her. She also wondered how things were going with Hannah. She put the thought out of her head when she heard the door open.

"Hey Eden," she heard a friendly female voice call out.

"Hey Hannah, hey Mikael. Take a seat anywhere. Do you need menus?"

"No, we know what we want," Mikael said.

So do I, Eden thought to herself, your brother. She didn't mention that Johnny had told her who he was, not knowing if Hannah was ready for anyone to know. After taking their order, she brought their drinks and waited for Max, her chef, to prepare their lunch. Maybe I should ask Hannah for some advice, Eden thought. She walked over to their table.

Looking at Hannah, she said, "Could I talk to you for a couple of minutes?"

"Of course."

Eden walked up front, Hannah right behind her.

"Could I trouble you for a little advice?" Eden asked.

"Let me guess, man trouble?"

"Yeah. I met a guy a little while back. He's new to town and became a regular. We started talking and hung out at his house a couple of times, just as friends. We told each other some personal stuff about our families and early life, then after our last dinner together, he stopped coming in or calling. If I did something, I don't know what."

"Were you clear it was just friends?"

"Yes, and that was his idea as well, so I know it's not that."

"Maybe his feelings changed, or he got scared. Is there anything in what he told you that could explain it?"

"Well, he told me that everyone he ever loved left him. He lost his wife to cancer and both his parents have passed his dad recently."

As soon as she said that, she regretted it.

"I'm sorry. I should have told you who I was talking about," Eden said.

"It's okay. I need to get used to it, so having you know helps."

"I understand if you don't want to continue talking about him."

"Not at all. I'm ready to talk with him about it, so this is helping. That could be it, especially if you two have gotten closer. Even though it's just as friends, he might still feel that fear. My advice, difficult as it may be, is to call and ask him."

"I leaned that way, but then thought maybe that would upset him more."

"I would suggest approach it from a place of concern, not hurt or anger, or he might feel cornered."

"Thank you. Sorry for pulling you away from your handsome man."

"No need to apologize. I'm always here if you need an ear."

With a smile on her face. Hannah headed back to her table. A few minutes later, Max let her know the food was ready, so Eden grabbed it and dropped it off. Watching Hannah and Mikael laughing and talking while they ate was giving her a brief pang. She missed hanging out and talking with Johnny. She decided she was going to follow Hannah's advice and call him later. She was just getting ready to clean up at the end of the night when she heard the door. She was hoping it wasn't someone wanting food, as she'd already sent Max home.

"Eden."

"Hi Johnny."

"Can we sit?"

Eden nodded and followed Johnny to his favorite table in the corner.

"I need to apologize," he said.

"No need. Is everything okay?"

"It's just my stupid fear."

"First off, it's not stupid, considering what you've been through. Second, know that you can always talk to me."

"That's the problem."

"I don't understand."

"I'm happy that we've become such good friends, and I don't want to lose you."

"I'm not going anywhere. I promise."

"You can't promise that. Katie promised she'd love me forever and look what happened."

"Nobody could have known she would become ill."

"It was my fault. If I hadn't let myself get close to her, she'd still be here."

"Oh Johnny, that's not true at all."

"It feels like it."

"I bet she'd be the first one to tell you it wasn't."

"I guess, but I still can't help but feel that way."

"Stand up," she requested.

Johnny stood, and Eden wrapped her arms around him. He returned her embrace, his breath catching in his throat. He loved the way she felt in his arms, as if she was born just for him to hold. He pulled away after a couple of minutes and sat back down.

"Thank you for listening. Can we give our friendship another chance?" he asked.

"It went nowhere. I'll always be here for you, whether you let yourself believe it."

"Okay."

"Now, I believe you still owe me an outing to the club. Tomorrow night is a karaoke night, so how about it? I have a night manager tomorrow, so I'll finish early."

"I'd love to."

"Great, now get your ass out of my way. I need to clean so I can get home."

As he always did when he was here at closing time, Johnny helped her, then walked her to her car. They shared a quick goodbye, and each headed home to rest up. Eden couldn't get her mind off Johnny. She was thankful she'd done nothing to upset him, but she felt bad that he was suffering so much. She hoped maybe he could find a way to just relax and enjoy their friendship.

Like Eden, Johnny was also thinking about his friend. He felt awful for ignoring her these past few weeks. His mind then wandered to what song they could sing together. He always wanted to try goofing around to Sonny and Cher's I Got You, Babe, so he decided he would suggest that one to Eden.

The next night, Johnny picked Eden up at her house, then they headed to the club.

"I was thinking about what we could sing tonight," Johnny announced.

"What did you come up with?"

"How about I Got You, Babe?"

"Ooh, I love that song."

"Great, I can't wait."

"Me either."

When they got inside, Eden saw Hannah and Mikael, along with another couple. She waved at Hannah before she and Johnny took a seat. Eden walked up to the bar and signed them up to sing. A few minutes later, a waiter stopped by to take their order.

"It's nice being waited on for a change."

"You deserve it, angel."

"Aww, you're sweet."

"Keep that to yourself. I'm supposed to be a badass drummer."

"Okay, our little secret."

"Thanks."

When Karaoke started, Hannah and Mikael were first up, the club's owner announcing her as a fan favorite. This was Eden's first time, so she had never heard Hannah sing, but when the music started, Eden and Johnny's jaws both dropped when they heard her incredible voice.

"Wow, she can sing," Eden said.

"She's amazing."

It was no surprise to Johnny, given his musical ability. He hoped someday Hannah would embrace the chance to build a relationship with him. She was the only family he had left. A few more people took their turn, then Johnny heard him and Eden get called to the stage. After locating their song, they started the music and grabbed their mikes. He hadn't yet heard Eden sing, and her voice impressed him. The whole time they sang, he couldn't take his eyes off her. They returned to their table as the crowd cheered their approval.

Once Karaoke was done, the club's DJ announced the dance floor was now open. After a few faster songs, the DJ slowed things down. Johnny had been thinking about the couple of times he and Eden had hugged, and he wanted to feel that again. The change in tempo gave him the perfect chance.

"Wanna dance?" he asked.

"I'd love to."

They walked to the dance floor and Johnny pulled Eden into his arms. She wrapped her arms around him and laid her head on his broad chest. As Johnny swayed with Eden in his arms, the rest of the room disappeared. He looked down at his beautiful friend and his heart started racing. There was little doubt in his mind that he was falling for her, but he was determined to keep fighting it. He just couldn't move past everyone leaving him, and he knew trying to get over losing Eden would send him over the edge.

Eden nestled herself into Johnny's embrace. There was something calming and safe when she was in his arms. She was also feeling a lot of butterflies flitting around her stomach. She was having feelings for him, and that scared the hell out of her. She hadn't let herself even think about getting close to another man after her marriage failed. Friendship would have to be enough, even if her lips wanted to taste his.

Johnny lowered his head closer to Eden's, inhaling the sweet scent of her strawberry shampoo. She was one of the most beautiful women he'd ever laid eyes on. All he could think about at that moment was kissing her sexy pink lips, not to mention the other parts of her body he knew would taste delicious. They stayed in each other's arms until the music sped up again, then returned to their table.

"It's been a long time since I've done that," Eden confessed.

"You enjoy dancing?"

"I always have. I especially wanted to learn ballroom and Latin dancing. I asked Todd once, but he told me it was ridiculous, so I never did it. I know I could have signed up alone, but I wanted to do it with someone I knew."

"Forgive me for saying this, but that guy did not deserve a woman like you."

"Thanks. I wish I'd been less concerned with making my parents happy and more concerned with my happiness. I never had my chance to have that bad-boy rock star romance I'd always dreamed of."

Johnny's eyebrows raised when he heard the last part. Could he be the one that made her fantasy come true? He knew for sure he wanted to. His resistance to a relationship was slipping away, and he wanted this woman. He knew what he needed to do.

They left the club a little before 10, as they both had to be up for work in the morning. Johnny pulled into her driveway, then walked her to her door. She couldn't get over what a gentleman he was, though a part of her wished he wasn't. She would love for him to grab her, pull her in close, and crush his lips to hers. She couldn't help but wonder what beautiful secrets were hiding under his clothes and pictured herself exploring his body with her tongue, her fingers, and anything else he wanted her to. She went inside, locked up and headed to bed, again wishing Johnny was lying right next to her.

The next morning, Johnny took his lunch hour and drove to City Ballroom Dance Studio.

"Good afternoon, sir. May I help you?" the woman at the desk asked.

"I'm interested in signing up for lessons. I want to surprise a special friend, so I'd like to pay for two."

"One moment please." She picked up the phone, and he heard her say, "I have a customer interested in signing up for classes." After a slight pause, she said, "thank you. She'll be right out, sir."

"Thank you."

A couple minutes later, the school's lead teacher greeted Johnny, who took him to her office. Once he explained what he wanted, she took care of getting him signed up and his payment processed. She handed him the class schedule and clothing and shoe requirements.

"You and your companion will need to fill out the releases included in your packet and bring it to your first class. We look forward to having you both join us."

"Thank you ma'am. I can't wait to surprise her."

She walked him out, and he headed back to work. Once he finished for the day, he walked over to The Garden of Eden to give Eden her surprise. She was a little busy when he arrived, so he sat down at his favorite table and waited until she had a break and could join him. She sighed when she sat down.

"Everything okay, Angel?"

"Busy day, so I haven't had a break until now. I haven't even had time to eat since breakfast."

"You must be starving. Are you able to leave soon?"

"Yes, I was just getting ready to head home."

"How about dinner first? I've been craving pizza and would love some company."

"I'd love to. Let me just make sure my night crew needs nothing."

"Take your time."

When she was ready, they each drove to Eden's favorite pizza place and went inside. The seating hostess took them to a table back in the corner. That was always Johnny's favorite place to sit, especially since he was often alone. He hated the thought of people sitting behind him and judging him for being a loser. Their waiter stopped by to take their drink order while they perused the menu.

"What do you like on your pizza?" Johnny asked.

"I like sausage," she flirted.

Johnny almost fell off his chair. There was a naughty woman inside that soft body, and he was dying to unleash her. He hoped the dance lessons would help her realize they belonged together. Their waiter returned with a beer for Johnny and a glass of wine for Eden. Johnny ordered a large pie with sausage. The waiter thanked them and headed to the kitchen to submit their order. While they waited, Johnny pulled an envelope out of his jacket pocket.

"I have a little surprise for you," he divulged.

"What is it?"

Johnny handed her the envelope and said, "I signed the two of us up for ballroom lessons."

"Oh my god," she squealed. "You want to do this?"

"I never thought I would dance, but after hearing you talk about it last night, I wanted you to get your wish."

"I don't know what to say, except thank you."

"My pleasure. All the information on what we need is in the envelope. There's a release form you need to fill out. The classes are every Sunday, so I hope that works with your schedule."

"It sure does. I'm so excited about this," she said, her eyes filling with tears.

"I didn't mean to make you sad," he said.

"I promise, you didn't. These are happy tears. Nobody's ever done anything like this for me. You're an amazing friend, and I'm so lucky you came into my life."

His heart sank a little hearing her refer to him only as a friend, and he hoped to change that. He wanted to at the very least take her on a date, but he doubted she would agree to that, so he said nothing.

"I know the weeknights are tough now that we're both working, but would you like to go to the club this Saturday night? We could practice some dance moves before we start class on Sunday. I don't want to look like a total idiot," he said.

"I'd love too. Maybe we could stop for Chinese on the way?"

"Sounds great."

The waiter brought their pizza over, along with another round of drinks. They were both famished and didn't leave a single slice on the plate. Eden still felt hungry and asked Johnny if he wanted to stop at the local diner for pie and coffee before they both went home. He agreed, so they met at the diner, each of them ordering a slice of pumpkin pie and a cup of decaf. They finished their dessert and both of them headed home to get some much-needed rest.

Chapter Seven

Even though he was seeing her every day during lunch, Johnny still called Eden Saturday morning to make sure they were still on for that night.

"I'm looking forward to dancing the night away."

"Me too. Would you like to have dinner with me before we head over, or do you just want to eat there?"

"If it's okay, I'd rather eat before we go."

"Sounds good. Anything special you're hungry for?"

I'm hungry for you, she thought to herself. "How about Italian?"

"My favorite. I'll pick you up at 5."

"Can't wait."

Johnny loved hearing Eden say she was excited about spending time with him. He was falling for her and hoped she was feeling the same for him. He went upstairs to shower and get dressed, opting for jeans and a black button-down shirt. He left a couple buttons open as he'd seen Eden checking out his chest a few times. He finished his outfit with black boots and a splash of Bulgari cologne before he drove to Eden's house. He knocked on the door, his jaw dropping when she answered.

Eden was a vision to behold. Like him, she was wearing jeans and a pair of boots, hers brown. Her forest green v-neck t-shirt looked especially beautiful against her blonde hair, not to mention the perfect amount of cleavage the shirt revealed. He could smell his new favorite scent, her strawberry shampoo, and his mouth started watering. He wanted this woman more than she could know. But did she feel that same about him?

After composing himself, he cooed, "You look stunning."

She blushed as she responded, "Thank you. You look pretty damn good yourself."

They walked over to his car, as Johnny again felt his heart beating out of his chest. This woman had a hold on him like nobody before her. It wasn't just her outer beauty that attracted him, it was also her kind heart and passionate soul. Not only was he falling for her, but he felt like he was falling in love with her, and he had to admit, it felt incredible, with a bit of fear mixed in.

"So, you said you wanted Italian. I'm still learning the different restaurants in the area, so I'm letting you pick."

"Pasquale's is my favorite."

Johnny entered that in his GPS and started heading toward the restaurant. The hostess seated them at a cozy table for two. Even though they were still just friends, this felt like a date to Johnny. He imagined what it would be like to start dating Eden. As it often did, his mind went right to sex. He tried not to picture what making love to her would be like, as he wanted just to experience it.

After they finished dinner, they rode to the club and went inside. Johnny noticed quite a few heads turn when they walked by, especially men when they caught sight of his angel. They found a table and ordered a couple of drinks before hitting the dance floor. A slow song started playing, and Johnny pulled her in close. His cologne was the sexiest thing she'd ever smelled, and it was having quite the impact on her body. She loved being in his arms and pictured him leaning his head down and kissing her. They ended up dancing the night away until they were both so spent they called it a night.

When Johnny pulled up in front of her house, he parked and walked her to her door. She gave him a hug and a quick peck on the cheek before she went inside. He felt like his face was on fire and he wanted more. He wanted more than anything to feel her lips on his, while her naked body was in his arms, his dick inside her. He'd make sure she never again had a lover who was a dud like her ex-husband. Once she was inside and he heard her door lock, he got back in his car and headed home.

He woke up the next morning, excited about their first class. He couldn't wait to see her dressed for class, especially in high heels. There was something about high heels that made a woman irresistible. Eden already was irresistible, he thought, so heels would just make her even hotter. He felt himself getting nervous as he drove to her house to pick her up for their class.

She opened the door when she saw his car and walked outside, locking the door behind her. Despite the weather being warm, she had a long coat on, hiding her outfit, but not her sexy shoes. She had on a pair of light blue heels with straps around the ankles. One look at them and his dick started stirring in his pants. He took a deep breath to calm himself before she reached his car. She got in and flashed a smile that could have melted all of Antarctica.

"Why the coat?" he asked.

"I didn't want anyone to see me."

"Why?"

"I don't look good in this dress."

"I bet you're wrong. You're going to have to take it off in class."

"I know."

When they got to the studio, she removed her coat and Johnny's eyes damn near popped out of his head like in those cartoons he watched as a kid. His angel stood before him in a long, flowing dress the same color as her shoes.

"Holy hell, you're stunning," Johnny complimented.

Eden's face turned bright red. "Thanks."

Johnny looked around the studio and noted there were five other couples in the class. He hoped he wouldn't look like an ass in front of them, and in front of Eden. Promptly at 3 PM, their instructor entered the studio.

"Good afternoon, and thank you for joining my class. My name is Rebecca. We'll be together for the next eight weeks, learning a different dance each week. At the end, there will be a showcase where you can dance in any of the styles we will learn. This week's class will start with the waltz. Before we begin, does anyone have questions?"

Nobody did, so Rebecca started by explaining the history of the dance. She then called in her teaching partner, a handsome man named Derek. They showed the hold and basic steps before instructing the couples to try it themselves. Johnny felt Eden's hand on his arm as she got herself into the hold position Rebecca showed them. Johnny got himself into the correct position and they started dancing. Rebecca stopped at each couple to check their progress. She smiled when she reached Eden and Johnny.

"Have you two done this before?" Rebecca asked.

"I haven't," Johnny said.

"Me either," Eden said.

"Well, you both appear to have a knack for this, and you're a stunning couple. How long have you been together?"

"We're just friends," Johnny said.

Raising her eyebrows, she said, "Well, keep up the good work."

Eden was having such a good time being twirled around the dance floor by Johnny, and she couldn't believe it when Rebecca announced their hour was up. She thanked them all for a great class, then left the studio. Johnny helped Eden into her coat, then they walked out to his truck.

"Would you like to hang out for a while, then maybe have some dinner?" he asked.

"I'd love to. Would it be okay if we stopped by my house so I can change?"

Johnny drove to her house and walked her inside.

"Thank you again for today. I had so much fun," she said, as she threw her arms around his neck.

Wrapping his arms around her waist, he pulled her in close. She looked up at him, gazing into his gorgeous green eyes. He locked eyes with her, the two of them just standing there looking at each other.

"You're the most beautiful woman I've ever known," he proclaimed.

"Hard to believe, given all the women you must have known."

"I promise you, I'm telling the truth. You are stunning, my angel."

"Thank you. You are quite handsome yourself," she cooed. "Would you like to practice our waltz before I get changed?"

He put a hand out. "May I have this dance?"

Taking his hand, she said, "Yes."

Johnny grabbed his cell and turned on some music. They got into the hold Rebecca showed in class and started dancing around her living room. She felt like she was riding on a cloud as she felt her feelings for Johnny move closer and closer to love. If only she possessed the courage to tell him, but given how he felt about relationships, she remained silent. The music stopped, so they stopped their dance as well, just standing and embracing.

Johnny lowered his head to hers and brushed her lips with his. He felt her open for him and deepened his kiss, sliding his tongue into her mouth. He pulled her tight to him as he felt her kissing him back. Needing to catch his breath, Johnny broke the kiss, but not his gaze into her eyes.

"I'm sorry, I don't know what came over me," he said.

"You didn't feel me try to stop you, did you?"

"No, I didn't."

Without another word, she crushed her lips to his, kissing him with even more passion than he had. This kiss also lasted a lot longer than the first until Johnny pulled away.

"I can't do this," he said.

"I don't understand."

"I told you I can't be in a relationship and you tempt me like this," he said.

"That's not fair. You kissed me first."

"It's because you wore that dress."

"I wore this dress, as that was what the paper said was appropriate for class."

"Just forget it. This can never happen again. We're friends and nothing more."

"But, Johnny."

"Don't. I'll see you for class, but that's all."

Before she could respond, Johnny stormed out, slamming the door behind him. She heard his tires screech as he raced out of her driveway.

She walked over to the couch and sat down, her face crumpling as her heart sank. She grabbed a pillow and clutched it against her chest as tears streamed down her cheeks. She couldn't understand what had happened. They were both enjoying the kiss. She hoped that after he calmed down, she'd hear from him, but that never happened.

A week went by and she was getting ready for their second dance class. She still hadn't heard from Johnny, so she drove herself to class. Today's dance is the Viennese waltz. Great, she thought, another romantic dance. She wore a similar dress as she had the week before, but had chosen a pastel pink dress and white shoes, her long blonde hair in a loose braid. She saw Johnny walk in, looking like his usual handsome self. He was wearing black pants and a white button-down shirt. She could see his tattoo through the thin fabric, and it was so sexy. She knew she should hate him after his outburst, but she just couldn't.

"Good afternoon, Eden."

"Hi Johnny."

He didn't say another word. She walked over to a chair and sat down, her mind returning to last Sunday. She tried to be mad at him for the way he yelled at her, but she knew it was fear and pain talking, not anything she did. She wanted nothing more than to throw her arms around him and let him know she'd never leave him. She wanted to kiss away his pain and just love him. She felt tears threaten to spill, and she wiped them away before class started.

Johnny was standing off to the side of the studio. He saw Eden raise her hand to her face and swipe at her eyes. Shit, he thought to himself, she's crying because of me. He wanted nothing more at that moment than to envelop her in his embrace and hold her close. He loved her and hated himself for how he treated her. So many times this past week, he thought about stopping by her restaurant to explain, but he was too embarrassed and couldn't bring himself to face her. A couple of minutes later, Rebecca and Derek walked in, so he joined Eden.

After explaining the dance and doing a demo, it was their turn. Eden stood and faced Johnny, both of them getting into proper position. As they danced to the romantic music, holding each other close, Johnny felt his resistance fading. He put his mouth near her ear.

"I'm sorry."

He saw tears form in her eyes.

"After class."

He nodded as they kept dancing. After having a week to beat himself up and regret how he treated her, it was time to come clean and tell what he hadn't yet. He hoped she would then understand why they could be nothing more than friends and things could go back to the way they were before he let his guard down and kissed her. Once class was over, they agreed to meet at their favorite diner.

"I need to explain what happened last week," Johnny announced.

"Yes, you do."

"Would it be okay if we went back to your house after we eat? I'd rather not talk about it here."

"I suppose, as long as you promise not to run out on me again."

"I do."

After they finished dinner, Johnny followed Eden to her house. Once they went inside, they sat down on her couch.

"I hope you know that my anger wasn't for you. I told you before about my wife and then my parents, but there've been so many more. Not one person who ever came into my life stayed. It wasn't all death. Some just left because they'd taken what they wanted and then threw me away. Nobody has ever wanted to stay in my life, and I can't face that again."

"I understand, but haven't I already proven I'm not going anywhere?"

"So far, yes, but it hasn't been that long."

"Let me prove it."

"I want to, but I just can't take the chance. Nobody knows what the future will bring."

"You're right, they don't, but we can't live our lives in fear. That's not living."

Johnny's face softened as he moved closer to her and wrapped her in his arms. He leaned in and kissed her, tenderly at first, then with more passion. He felt her open for him and slid his tongue into her mouth. She twirled her tongue with his, wrapping her arms around his neck as they kissed. Eden moaned, the sweetest sound he'd ever heard. He stopped the kiss.

"Are you okay?" she asked.

"I need to say something before I lose my courage."

"Okay."

"I'm in love with you."

"Oh, Johnny. I'm in love with you, too."

"I wanna make love to you. When you're ready, of course."

Without saying another word, Eden stood and held out her hand. She led him to her bedroom, wrapping her arms around him when they got inside. He pulled her in close, his heart soaring.

"Please take me to bed."

"Are you sure?"

"More sure than I've ever been in my life. I want you, Johnny," she cooed.

Johnny unzipped her dress, letting it fall to the floor. His heart started racing when he saw her standing there in light pink lingerie. He'd never seen a more beautiful sight than this amazing woman. He looked down when he felt her fingers opening the buttons on his shirt and removing it. She got to see his tattoo in all its glory, and she couldn't wait to hear the story behind it. Right now, though, she was interested in other parts of his body!

She opened his belt, then unfastened his pants, letting them fall to his ankles. He kicked off his shoes, removed his socks, then kicked his pants off. She slid her fingers inside the waistband of his sexy black briefs and slid them down. One look at his dick and her eyes went wide. Damn, he was huge. She couldn't wait to feel that, feel him, inside her.

He pulled her close and removed her bra. She could feel his dick pressing against her as he lowered her thong. She stepped out of it and kicked it aside. Even that move was sexy, he thought to himself. He scooped her up and carried her over to her bed, laying her down. He laid down next to her and pulled her into his arms, kissing her hard. Her soft skin felt incredible against his as they kissed. She ran her fingers through his hair, sending chills down his entire body.

His hands went a journey down her back, her bottom, then her leg. She watched as he opened her legs, gasping when she felt him slide a couple of fingers inside her. She moaned as he slid his fingers in and out.

She had almost forgotten how good it felt to be touched. Her moaning got louder when he started rubbing her swollen bud.

"Mmm, it feels so good," she purred.

"I want to taste every inch of you, my angel."

Starting with her neck and working his way down to her thighs, he showered her body with soft kisses, smiling when he saw her spread her legs wider. He wanted to taste her there more than anywhere else. After running his tongue up and down her sexy inner thighs as she writhed beneath him, he ran his tongue inside her folds, stopping at her clit. Her breathing became shallower as she moaned louder. He didn't stop until her entire body started quaking as she cried out at the intense pleasure, the most beautiful music he'd ever heard.

"Oh, Johnny, I need you inside me. Please."

Covering her body with his, he slid inside her pussy, still slick from her orgasm. No woman he'd ever been with felt as good as his angel. It was as if the universe made them for each other. He slid in and out of her incredible body as she accepted every inch of him inside her. She wrapped her arms around him, her nails raking his back as they became one. One body. One heart. One soul. She felt his pace increase as he neared his climax, growling like a lion.

"Please. Johnny, please come inside me."

"Oh baby. I love you so much," he said as he emptied inside her.

He laid on his back next to her, smiling as she moved closer to him, laying her head on his chest. He wrapped her in his arms, holding her tight against him.

"No man has ever made me feel the way you just did."

"You're by far the most amazing woman I've ever been with," he professed. "I love you more than I ever knew was possible. I never thought I'd be able to give my heart to another until a beautiful angel with hair of gold danced into my life."

"Oh, Johnny. I love you. You've awakened something inside me I forgot even existed. Nobody's ever touched me with such passion. You are by far the most incredible lover I've ever had, and while it's true that I've only had a few partners in my life, I would feel the same if I'd had hundreds."

Johnny caressed her cheek with his strong fingers, as he crushed his lips to hers. He wanted her so much, his dick regained its erection. He pulled her on top of him. She sat up, taking his length inside her, sliding her sweet pussy up and down his cock. His powerful hands held her back, supporting her as she rode him. He watched in awe as her beautiful breasts bounced. She threw her head back, screaming as his dick connected with her g-spot and clit with every powerful thrust.

He could hear her breathing change as she neared climax, nearing that beautiful peak himself. She cried out in pure, unbridled ecstasy as her body erupted. He joined her, coming inside her as she constricted around him, wave after wave of intense pleasure consuming both their bodies. As soon as she could move, she laid next to him as they held each other tight. He heard the soft snoring and smiled as he looked at this beautiful woman sleeping in his arms. He pulled the covers up, then drifted off himself, neither of them stirring until morning.

Chapter Eight

Monday morning made its unwelcome appearance, though this one wasn't so bad. She woke up in Johnny's arms, making this the least-Mondayest Monday Eden had in a while. She stretched her arms as Johnny also awakened.

"Good morning, my beautiful angel."

"Mmm, good morning, my sexy Roman god."

"So you know who that is," he said, pointing at his tattoo.

"Of course, it's Julius Caesar. I'm curious what the meaning behind it is."

"I'm guessing you know veni, vidi, vici or I came, I saw, I conquered."

"I do."

"I got that after signing a record deal and moving to LA. Although music ended up not working out, I still did it. What I haven't told you yet is the deep stage fright I had to overcome to even set foot behind my drum kit. I fought through that and the fear went away."

"That's amazing. Thank you for sharing that with me. I find the tattoo pretty damn sexy, especially on your hot chest."

She looked up at him and brushed her soft lips against his. That was all it took, and he was hard.

"Mmm, someone else just woke up," she purred.

"Thanks to that sweet mouth."

"Not always sweet."

"Oh? Prove it."

Flashing her sexy smile, she said, "Let's fuck. I wanna slide my pussy down on that hard cock. I'm so fuckin' wet for you."

Johnny's jaw dropped. She had yet to give him a taste of her dirty talk until now. He still couldn't believe she had been with a man who didn't like that. Hearing those words escape her lips left him groaning, his dick aching to be inside that beautiful pussy.

"Come to me, baby."

She climbed on top, taking him in deep. She leaned back, using his strong thighs to support herself as she rode him. He ran his hands up the length of her body, stopping to massage her breasts.

"So good, baby," he said.

He grabbed her hips, allowing her to fuck him even harder. She came undone, soaking his dick with her powerful orgasm. He loved the way she looked on top of him, body quaking as she kept riding. She worked herself into another frenzy, even more powerful than the last. This time, Johnny exploded with her as they climaxed together. She collapsed onto his chest as he held her close.

"Baby, I need to hear more of that dirty talk when we're in bed. That was so damn hot," Johnny said.

"I promise there's plenty more where that came from. But right now, I need to get ready for work."

"Me too. How about we grab a shower together? You know, to save time."

"For the sake of saving time, I suppose I can suffer through showering with the sexiest man I've ever met."

She got up and started walking toward her bathroom, Johnny close behind, his eyes never leaving her sexy little ass. Johnny's eyes scanned her bathroom, with its rich plum colored walls, soaking tub, and walk-in shower. They stepped into the stall and Eden turned on the water. Johnny held her close, kissing her as hot water streamed down their bodies. Johnny had to use her shower gel, loving the fact that he would carry her sweet scent with him all day.

When they got out of the shower and back into her bedroom,

Johnny realized he had no clothes there except what he was wearing the day before. Not wanting to put dirty clothes back on, he had to go with just his coat and get dressed when he got home.

"Guess we'll have to leave some stuff at each other's house, so this doesn't happen next time," she said.

"There's going to be a next time?"

"I hope there's lots of them."

"I give you my word."

"I'd rather have your dick."

"Who are you and what did you to do with Eden?"

"You've awakened the beast. No going back now."

"More like the beauty. For now, though, I need to get home and dressed if I have a chance of getting to work on time."

"I need to finish getting ready as well. Can we see each other tonight?"

"Of course."

He kissed her goodbye and headed to his car. She stood at her front door, watching her sexy man drive away. She walked back inside, somewhat in disbelief at what she just experienced. He was everything she'd ever hoped a lover would be. She floated around her house as she finished getting ready, then left for work herself. The restaurant was already open as she arrived later than usual. Max had a concerned look on his face, as Eden was always early. That look turned to amusement when he looked at her face.

"You had sex," he announced.

"What? How can you tell? I mean, no I didn't."

"You can't fool me. I've never seen you look as happy as you do this morning. That smile wouldn't have anything do to with a certain drummer, would it?"

Eden tried to scowl, but her face had other ideas and she couldn't wipe the smile off her face.

"Promise me you'll keep this between us. It's new and the journey to get here hasn't been easy for either of us, so I just don't want to make a big thing of it."

"I get it, and you have my word. I'm happy for you, you deserve this."

"Thanks, Max."

He nodded and returned to the kitchen as customers were filing in. Eden took food orders and sent them to the kitchen, pouring coffee as they waited. Max was a skilled cook and always turned orders around quickly. Eden had become known for her quick but delicious breakfast, thanks in part to Hannah handing out fliers to her store's patrons. The afternoon flew by and a little before she was getting ready to call it a day, her cell rang. A huge grin spread across her face when she saw Johnny's name on her caller ID.

"Hey, sexy, she said.

"Mmm, my gorgeous angel."

"How about my place tonight? I've been dreaming of having you in my bed."

"That sounds fun. I just need to stop home and pack a few things, assuming you want me to spend the night."

"Oh yes, I want you so bad. I've had a hell of a time focusing today."

Looking around to make sure nobody was in earshot, she said, "My pussy's so wet for you, baby. I can't wait to feel you inside me tonight."

"Holy fuckin' shit, you're so damn sexy."

"Just you wait, my sexy badass drummer."

"I just pulled into my driveway. Please get here NOW."

"On my way, stud."

She disconnected and said goodbye to Max. He winked in return, an amused look on his face. She walked out to her car, stopped home to pack a change of clothes and some toiletries, then raced over to Johnny's house. She couldn't wait to see his bedroom. She couldn't wait to lie naked in his bed. She had written countless sex scenes filled with steamy desire and passion, but until she met Johnny, she'd never experienced it for herself. Just thinking about his hands and his mouth on her skin drove her wild. She had a little something in mind for tonight, something she'd never done before.

Johnny heard her car pull in, so he opened the door. She almost crashed her car when she saw him standing there in just lounge pants. She would never tire of gawking at that sexy chest, her panties soaked just from looking at him. He walked outside and grabbed her bag, his arm around her waist as they walked inside.

She looked at his kitchen table, smiling when she saw a pizza, along with a glass of wine for her and a beer for him. Also new to the table was a bouquet of sunflowers.

"How did you know sunflowers are my favorite?"

"Your bathroom decor."

"I'm impressed. Todd never noticed a damn thing. Sorry, I shouldn't be mentioning my ex."

"It's okay. I'm not intimidated by him after the stories you told me."

"There's one other thing I wanted to mention, but I'm afraid you'll make fun of me."

"I promise I won't."

"There's something I always wanted to do to him, but he thought it was nasty."

"What?"

"Oral. When you did that to me the other night, it was the first time anyone ever had."

"So, my dick would be the first ever to feel those soft lips?"

"Yes."

"Now I know for sure I'll never have to worry about you going back to him."

"Just you wait until later when I show you how little you need to worry."

"And just what do you have in mind?"

"You'll have to wait and see."

He stood and held out his hand to help her up. Without warning, he picked her up and threw her over his shoulder. He felt her hands smacking his ass as he carried her to his bedroom, setting her down when they were inside.

"You're in trouble now," she said.

"Punish me, baby."

Flashing him the most wicked look he'd ever seen, she said, "Get naked and get your hot ass on that bed."

"Fuck, baby."

"Less talking, more stripping. I don't have all night. Well, I do, but I don't like to be kept waiting."

Who was this woman, he thought to himself, and why did it take me this long to find her? Once he was naked, he laid down as she demanded. She grabbed her phone and a minute later, Johnny heard Closer by Nine Inch Nails play. That song was already one of the sexiest songs he'd ever heard, but his woman took it up about a million notches. She stripped for him, her hands running all over her body, his dick standing at full attention.

After she was naked, she crawled onto the bed, got on all fours, and wrapped her soft lips around his dick. She wasn't sure what to expect, but she loved having him in her mouth. She slid her lips up and down his cock, running her tongue along his shaft as she sucked. She let her fingers tease his balls, feeling his chest heave.

"Fuck, baby, so damn good."

"I wanna taste you," she purred.

She sucked him harder, her beautiful hand cupping his balls as he lost all control and filled her mouth. She locked eyes with him and swallowed him down, licking her lips to make sure she didn't waste any.

"Delicious," she purred.

"I thought I was getting punished?"

"You are. You're going to do as I say for the rest of the night."

"Fuck, angel. What do you want now?"

"Get that tongue in my pussy and make me scream your name."

She laid on her back and spread her legs wide. I'll never tire of seeing her naked, he thought to himself. He lowered his head between those sexy legs and ran his tongue inside her sweet folds. Wrapping his lips around her swollen clit, he sucked her hard. He felt her fingers running through his hair, as loud moans escaped her beautiful lips. He slid a couple of fingers inside her as he sucked her pussy. Her body bucked beneath him, her sexy tits bouncing hard as she moved closer to the edge.

"OH FUCK JOHNNY!"

He continued his tongue lashing, making her come over and over, each time more powerful than the last. He increased the pressure of his fingers inside her while he kept sucking her clit until she drenched his hand.

"Johnny, holy fuck, oh Johnny, so fucking good. Now, get that cock inside me."

He slid up her body, sliding his dick inside her soaking wet pussy. He was so turned on from seeing her squirt, he pounded her pussy hard. She raked her nails down his back, then grabbed his ass, trying to pull him in even deeper.

"On your back now. I wanna ride you."

He wrapped his arms around her and rolled over, pulling her on top of him. She sat up straight, giving him a full view of her sexy body as she bounced on his cock. He filled her pussy with his hot cream as she exploded, her pussy tightening around him.

She climbed off and laid down next to him. Chests heaving and drenched in sweat, they laid together, basking in the afterglow of incredible passion. She was getting used to being in his arms, so grateful to be with someone passionate, someone with whom she could be herself. Johnny had awakened that wild child she kept hidden for so long, and it was beyond freeing.

"Can I ask you something personal?" Eden asked.

"Okay."

"Tell me if this is none of my business, but is Katie's illness the reason you left music behind?"

"It is. Once her doctor told us she was terminal, I couldn't go on tour. I had to be there for her."

"You're a special man."

"No. I'm not. I did what was right."

She caressed his cheek. "Well, I think you're special for sacrificing your dream for someone you love. Maybe it's time to pursue it."

"It's not practical. I need to have an income."

"Who says you can't with music? Promise me you'll think about it."

"I promise. Can I ask you something now?"

"Sure."

"Why did you marry Todd?"

"You're right. I was tired of being ignored and ostracized by my family, and I knew that marrying Todd would get me back in their good graces. It worked, too, until I left him. Although he cheated with my fucking sister, I was the one who brought disgrace by divorcing him. I haven't heard a peep from them since."

"I'm sorry, baby."

"It's been hard having no friends or family, but then something amazing happened."

"What?"

"I met you. For the first time in my life, I'm in love."

"I'm in love with you, baby. And now, I'm going to show you just how much."

"Oh, Johnny," she said.

She felt him crush his lips to hers, his tongue exploring her mouth. She wrapped her arms around him and pulled him close. He ran his tongue down her neck, then between her breasts. He sucked on her breasts one at a time, biting her nipples. The sweet sting left her moaning. He dragged his tongue down her body, stopping just short of her pussy, sending chills down her entire body.

"Mmm, I need you inside me," she purred.

Johnny moved on top of her, settling himself between her legs. Her breath caught in her throat when he entered her. He held her tight, kissing her as they made love. She loved the way he felt inside her, especially when he was moving his dick in and out. He angled her so his cock rubbed her clit with each thrust. Lost in the passion of their lovemaking, their bodies took flight like two birds soaring through the night sky. She felt him come inside her as she exploded beneath him. When they were done, he collapsed on the bed next to her. She giggled when her stomach growled.

"Hungry, baby?"

"Famished."

They put on robes and went out to the kitchen to have some dinner. They made up plates of leftovers and walked out to the living room to watch TV. When they finished eating, Johnny put his arms around Eden. She laid her head on his shoulder.

"I need to tell you something else about my failed marriage," she said.

"What, baby?"

"I should have told you this sooner, and I hope this won't change how you feel about me."

"No way anything could. I love you."

Tears appeared in her beautiful eyes as she said, "I can't have children. I hope that's not a deal breaker for you."

"No way, my angel."

"My family, Todd, and his family hated me for it. They blamed me as if it was my choice. Right after that is when he started sleeping with my sister."

"Baby, you didn't deserve any of that treatment. I'm so sorry they put you through that. Nobody is ever going to hurt you again."

"Thank you. I love you, Johnny."

"I love you, babe."

They spent the rest of the night snuggled on the couch, watching TV before heading off to bed.

Chapter Nine

The next couple of weeks flew by as both Eden's restaurant and Hannah's shop were busy with tourists. She and Johnny spent every night together. Most of those were nights they were naked, drenched in sweat and other fluids. Eden had a lot of years of boring sex to make up for, and Johnny was more than willing to drive her wild. She started thinking about some stories she'd written and wanted to try something new. Problem was, she feared saying something, afraid of what Johnny would think of her. She came up with a naughty little plan. They were sitting in the living room one night after dinner when Eden handed him a small stack of paper.

"What's this?" he asked.

"You mentioned wanting to read some of my work, so I thought I'd start with this."

She whispered, watching Johnny's face as he read. His jaw dropped further and further as he read her naughty words. He looked at her when he was done, unable to form words. When he regained his composure, he attempted to speak.

"Damn, baby, that's the hottest thing I've ever read. Have you ever been tied up?"

"Um, do you need to ask that with everything else I've told you?"

"Good point. So, would you want to? Get tied up, I mean?"

"I need to confess something. I've been thinking about it, but I was afraid to say anything."

"Why would you be afraid?"

"I was afraid you'd think less of me, so I tested your reaction by giving you that scene to read."

"Think less of you? No way in hell, just the opposite. I'm even more turned on by you. I think you better get that hot ass into the bedroom now."

Much to Johnny's amusement, she ran into the bedroom. He followed her in and sat down in the chair across from the bed.

"Get naked. NOW," he said.

She gazed into his eyes as she removed her clothes. She smiled when she saw him licking his lips. She turned it up a notch and ran her hands over her naked skin as she removed her clothes. When she was out of her jeans and panties, she took her hand and ran it down her stomach until her fingers were on her pussy. She threw her head back and moaned as she rubbed her clit.

"Get that naughty naked body in the middle of the bed and close your eyes."

She did as Johnny commanded. As she laid there, not knowing where he was or what he was doing, her heart was beating out of her chest. She'd wanted to try this for so long, and she was glad she had the guts to say something. She felt the bed move under Johnny's weight. He lifted her head and placed a blindfold on her. He took her wrists one at a time and tied her to the bed.

"Get ready baby. You're in for a wild ride."

"Oh, Johnny."

Starting at her feet, he slid his hands up her legs, teasing her skin before spreading her legs wide. She felt his tongue running up and down her inner thighs, driving her wild. Her pussy was throbbing with desire, aching for his touch, but he stayed on her legs. He started sucking as she tugged against her restraints, writhing beneath him. She wanted his tongue on her pussy.

"Please, baby, I need to feel you pleasure my pussy."

"I'm in charge tonight, so I'll decide when it's time to taste that sweet honey."

"Oh, baby," she purred.

She felt him slide up her body and started sucking her breasts. He ran his tongue over her rock-hard nipples as she tried to grind her pussy against him. She was so fucking wet.

"You better behave or I'm never gonna touch that pussy."

She laid still, a huge smile on her face as she felt him slide back down, dragging his tongue on her soft, warm skin. She felt his warm breath between her legs. She was so hot for him, she couldn't stand it. She felt his tongue between her folds, running up to her swollen clit.

"Oh, Johnny, so good."

He took her bud between his lips and sucked hard, then nipped her. The pleasure was like nothing she'd ever felt and she screamed. He kept sucking hard as her body bucked off the bed. He felt her quake as she came undone. He slid a couple of fingers inside, still sucking even after she came. He wouldn't stop sucking, no matter how many orgasms she had until she cried out.

"Baby, I can't take it anymore. Holy shit."

He ignored her and wouldn't remove his mouth from her, loving the taste of her sweet honey. He stopped and slid up her body. she felt his lips crush to hers as he slid his dick inside her. She loved feeling his long, thick cock filling her. She was so sensitive from what he'd just done to her that even his slow, gentle thrusts were threatening to send her soaring again. She loved hearing his groans as his dick moved in and out of her body, his hands lifting her hips off the bed and massaging her ass. She ached to touch him, run her fingers through his gorgeous hair, but she couldn't.

"Oh, fuck, my angel, I love you," he said as he filled her with his salty goodness.

"Oh, Johnny, I love you so much."

He untied her wrists and removed her blindfold, then laid down next to her.

"Baby, tell me how that felt," he said.

"I don't think there are enough words to give it justice. I've never experienced anything like that. I felt like I was floating on a cloud with my first orgasm. The longer you kept sucking on me, the more it felt like a thunderstorm."

"A thunderstorm? Is that a good thing?"

"Oh yes. Every suck and nip on my clit felt like a jolt of electricity through my body, and it felt incredible. My screams definitely rivaled thunder. Having my hands restrained and not being able to see anything let me focus even more on the pleasure and, oh my god, there was so much pleasure."

"Mmm, I am to please."

"Just you wait until I return the favor."

"And when will that be?"

"Guess you'll have to wait and see. But right now, I'm exhausted."

"I'm spent myself."

They got ready for bed and were sound asleep the minute their heads hit the pillow. They slept in the next morning, then enjoyed some delicious French toast Johnny whipped up.

"Damn, you cook in the kitchen and the bedroom, Mr. Sexy."

"Anything for you, my sexy little devil."

"I was wondering about something. Since we don't have any plans for Independence Day, I had an idea. I would love to have a barbecue for those who need a helping hand and give them a free meal. Would you like to help me?"

"Baby, you're amazing. It's my honor to help you."

"How about when we finish, we head down and start cooking so we have most of it ready, then all we have to do is grill the meat in the morning?"

"Sounds perfect."

After they finished eating, they headed down to the restaurant and cooked together well into the evening. Once everything was ready, they packed all the food into the walk-in refrigerator. While she was finishing up, Johnny walked out to the front and turned on some music. Eden came out and saw him standing there, a rose in his sexy mouth.

Handing her the rose, he said, "Dance with me, baby."

He took her into his arms, swaying to the music, loving how this amazing woman felt in his arms. She could feel his dick stirring in his jeans, soaking her panties. She lifted her head and kissed him hard, jamming her tongue into his mouth. She moaned as she felt him intertwine his tongue with hers.

"I need you to take me home right now," she said.

"And why are we so eager to get home?"

"Now that we've handled all that meat, I want you to handle yours."

"Oh, fuck, woman. Let's go!

Eden locked up the restaurant, then they raced to his truck and sped home. A trail of clothes marked the path from the living room to his bedroom. She threw him down on the bed, climbed on top of him, and took his dick inside her. They fucked hard and fast, both of them exploding, fueled by the heat of their shared passion and far too many years of being alone. She collapsed on him, both of their chests heaving. He wrapped his arms around her as she lowered her head and kissed him hard.

"I haven't yet christened the hot tub in my bathroom. Care to join me?"

"Ooh, that sounds like fun," she said.

Johnny turned on the heat to warm the water, then helped Eden climb in. He turned on the jets, then got in and sat next to her. She nestled against him, her head on his broad shoulder. They sat, enjoying the relaxing jets and especially each other's company. He looked down at his beautiful angel, vowing that nothing would ever come between them. He loved this woman, and he never wanted to spend another day without her.

"I guess we should get to bed," he said.

"Yes, we have a busy day tomorrow."

They got out of the tub, dried off and got in bed.

"Thank you again for helping me tomorrow," she said.

"My pleasure."

They kissed, then drifted off to sleep. Eden's cell phone alarm rang way too early, but she knew she had to get moving. As she was getting out of bed to grab a shower, Johnny woke up. They showered together, then got dressed and headed down to the restaurant. After a quick bite, they started getting all the chafing dishes set up so they could warm the food before people started arriving.

Eden rented a large grill, tents, long tables, and folding chairs so they could accommodate more people. After getting all the food warming up, they set up the tables and chairs and put out some decorations. She had contacted all the area's shelters to spread the word and by noon, she had quite a line. She and Johnny, along with some volunteers from the local high school, served food to everyone who came through the line. It warmed Eden's heart to see total strangers sitting down to enjoy a meal together.

Much to Eden's surprise, she had the owners of several other local restaurants stop by and drop off food donations. Their generosity ensured that she didn't have to turn anyone away, as there was more than enough food. They stayed until their guests ate every meal. Her volunteers stayed and helped clean up. When they were done, Eden thanked them all and let them know to reach out if they needed their hours verified.

"Thank you for including me," Johnny said.

"Thank you for the help. It made this whole day even more special that we did this together."

"Now that we're done, how about I make us some dinner? Johnny asked.

"Sounds great."

Johnny was about to dig through the refrigerator to see what he wanted to make when they heard the door open.

"When I told my mom what you were doing today, she insisted I bring you both some food," Max said.

He put the bag he was carrying on the counter and motioned for them to sit down. He made them each a plate and served them.

"Thank you, Max, for serving us, and please thank your mother for this thoughtful gesture," Eden said.

"She was happy to do it. She is a big believer in giving back. Now, you two, enjoy your meal and, of course, each other," he winked. He waved and headed out.

They dug into the meals that Max's mom prepared, both of them moaning as they devoured the food.

"I now know where Max got his skills in the kitchen," Eden said between bites.

"For sure, this food is incredible."

They finished eating so they could clean up and head home, both of them exhausted from a long, busy day. They passed out the minute

Johnny turned off the light, neither stirring until the sun poured through his windows.

With the beautiful summer weather, tourists continued to pour into the area, and Eden was working harder than ever. She was so exhausted every night that their sex life was cooling off. Johnny missed her warm, naked skin, so he hatched a plan. When Eden got to work the next morning, Max's mom was at a table eating some breakfast. When Eden saw her dining companion, she scrunched her forehead and approached the table.

"Okay, what are you up to?" Eden asked Johnny.

"You've been working so hard lately and you need a break."

"This is my business. I can't take a break."

"I figured you'd say that, so I called in reinforcements."

Max walked out of the kitchen and said, "I can handle things while you're gone."

"I know, but you can't cook and also handle the front."

"He won't be," Max's mom said. "I have plenty of experience running a restaurant and I'm tired of sitting home."

"I took this week off work, and you are now officially off as well," Johnny said.

Realizing this was a losing battle, she agreed. After thanking Max and his mother, he ushered Eden out the door and followed her home.

"Pack yourself a week's worth of clothes, then meet me at my house."

When Eden got to Johnny's, there was a note on the door instructing her to come in. She opened the door, noticing all the lights were off except for a glow coming from the bathroom. She could also hear music playing. Johnny was nowhere to be found, but she saw a series of papers with arrows and hearts drawn on them, directing her to the bathroom. She walked down to the bathroom and couldn't believe her eyes when she looked inside. Candles lined the entire hot tub platform. Johnny sat in the tub, a bottle of wine and two glasses next to him on a small table.

"Please take your clothes off and join me, my love," Johnny said.

"With pleasure."

She stripped for him, smiling as he bit his lower lip, never taking his eyes off her. He held out his hand to help her into the tub. Once she got comfortable, he poured two glasses of wine and handed one to her.

"To us and a week of relaxation, my angel. I love you," Johnny said.

"Cheers."

After clinking glasses, they each took a sip of wine, then put their glasses down.

"To what do I owe this pampering?" Eden asked.

"I've missed you, missed us."

"What do you mean? We've been together every night."

"But we haven't made love. Baby, I've missed feeling your soft skin against mine, missed being inside you. Though I don't want to see your health suffer if you don't take time to unwind."

"I'm sorry."

"No need to apologize. I'm not at all mad. Rather, I love you and I want to take care of you."

"I understand. I'm just not used to someone caring for me this way. Though, I'm enjoying it. Now, I believe you said something about making love."

She moved closer to him and turned his head toward hers. She leaned in and brushed her lips against his. He opened his mouth, so she deepened the kiss, sliding her tongue in his mouth. He returned her kiss as his hands explored her body. She moved onto his lap and kissed him again. Wrapping his arms around her, he leaned his head and sucked her sexy tits, flicking his tongue over her hard nipples. Fuck, he'd missed this.

He moved his hands to her ass, squeezing hard as she started grinding her pussy against his now-hard cock. She took every inch of his incredible cock deep inside her body, sliding her pussy up and down his hard shaft. She felt his hand connect with her ass and moaned.

"I've been a very naughty girl," she purred.

She loved the way it felt when he spanked her. She bounced on his cock hard, her tits bouncing in his face as he went back to squeezing her ass. He growled at every stroke of her hot pussy and grabbed her waist, lifting her up and down onto his cock.

"Fuck, Johnny, so good, baby. Oh fuck," she said as she came undone, drenching his cock as she came hard.

"Fuck, you're so hot, woman."

"Mmm. I wanna feel you come on my tits, baby," she said.

"Bed, NOW."

They got out of the tub, raced to his bedroom, not even bothering to dry off. Johnny straddled his sexy goddess and put his dick between her breasts. She grabbed her tits and pushed them against his dick, watching as he fucked them.

"Oh fuck, Eden, you're so damn naughty."

He darted to the bathroom and grabbed a towel to clean her up.

"I wanna see you on all fours, baby," he said.

He got on his knees behind, sliding his dick into her pussy. His hands on her hips, he fucked her, sliding in and out of her, his eyes glued to that sexy ass of hers. She was so felt so damn good wrapped around his dick, her body at the perfect angle to hit her g-spot hard. He starting thrusting harder until he felt her drench his dick as he emptied himself inside her. He flopped down next to her as she rolled onto her back, her body pressed against his.

"Damn, I missed that, baby."

"Mmmm, me too. Thank you for making me take some time off."

"My pleasure."

"Just you wait to see how pleasure you get this week, my sexy man."

After a quick nap, they went to the park and take a picnic lunch. Eden couldn't remember the last time she'd taken days off. It never used to bother her, as working kept her mind off being alone. Now that she was with Johnny, though, she was grateful for the time alone with him. Like him, she missed having sex and planned on more than making up for that this week. They had just arrived at the park and found a table when they saw Hannah and Mikael.

"I'm glad to see you could get Eden to take some time off," Hannah said.

"It took a bit of help. Thank you both for giving me some time off," Johnny said.

"Of course. We need to take care of our gorgeous women," Mikael said.

"We can take care of ourselves, thank you," Eden said..

"And don't you forget it," Hannah said.

Hannah and Mikael stayed for a couple more minutes before walking to one of the other empty tables.

"That's the first time she's said anything to me other than work-related stuff."

"Maybe she's finally coming to terms with having a brother."

"I hope so. There's so much I want to talk with her about. We both have a parent we never got to know. I want to learn about my birth mother and tell her anything she wants to know about our father."

"I can't imagine what either of you is going through, but I will be here for anything you need."

They stayed in the park for the rest of the afternoon, enjoying the beautiful weather. Johnny had his arm around her as they sat gazing at each other. He was about to kiss her when he saw all the color drain from her face. He saw her staring at something, so he turned to look and saw a man about their age headed their way. From her reaction, he didn't need to ask her who he was.

Chapter Ten

"Well, well, well, look who it is," Todd said.

"What the hell do you want?"

"That's all you can say after what you put me through?"

"I beg your pardon?"

"You embarrassed me by leaving me like that," he said, raising his voice.

Hannah and Mikael heard him and turned to look. They stood but stayed at their table for now. Hannah liked Eden, and she didn't want to see anyone upset her, so they watched them.

"What about the stuff you did to me?" Eden asked.

Johnny couldn't believe how calm she was. He watched her, but he didn't want to jump in unless she needed him to. One thing he knew for sure was this woman could take care of herself.

"Well, if you would have done what you were supposed to do, none of this would have happened. I mean, how pathetic of a woman do you have to be to not be able to have children? At least your parents had one worthwhile child."

Johnny couldn't believe what he just heard, and was about to jump in, thinking it would devastate Eden. He was dead wrong. Her ashen face turned bright red. She stood up straight and clenched her fists.

"Who the fuck do you think you are?" she said.

"I'm a man who knows how to behave in public, that's who."

"Not having children was out of my hands. A real man would have supported his wife, but not you. What did you do? You fucked my sister."

"You're making a scene."

"You started this, not me. What did you think? That I'd sit here and take it? Guess you never knew me then."

"And who's this clown?" Todd asked, nodding toward Johnny.

"This clown, as you referred to him, is only the kindest, sexiest, most exciting, most passionate man I've ever met. All things you know shit about," she said.

"Lower your voice. You're embarrassing me."

"Oh, boo hoo. Is your precious little reputation on the line? Well, let me tell everyone who's listening what else is little."

"Eden," Todd warned.

"You have the smallest dick I've ever seen. Or should I say couldn't see," she screamed at the top of her lungs.

Johnny saw Todd raise his hand. He got about halfway to Eden's face when Johnny's fist connected with his face.

"You will never hurt her again," Johnny said.

Todd's face turned bright red. He got up and stormed off without so much as another word. Johnny wrapped his arms around Eden as her body started shaking, tears streaming down her face. Mikael and Hannah walked over to lend their support. Everyone in the park was standing there gaping at them after that scene.

Hannah took Eden's hand and said, "Let's walk over to the restroom away from all these busy-bodies and get you cleaned up."

"I would have done the same thing if someone raised a hand to Hannah," Mikael said to Johnny.

"I saw red when I saw his hand headed for her face. I just hope she won't be mad at me."

"The way he was talking to her, I don't think she could be mad at you."

"Thanks."

"Before they get back, I need to say something to you."

"Okay."

"I know we've said little after you told Hannah about being her brother. Thank you for being patient with her."

"I understand the shock. I sat in the lawyer's office dumbfounded when I found out."

"I think she's getting close to being ready to talk, so just give her a little more time."

"As much as she needs."

"Thanks."

Johnny saw the ladies heading back, so he and Mikael walked over to meet them. Eden had stopped crying and had a smile on her face.

"Thank you," she said to Hannah.

Hannah grabbed Mikael's hand and nodded toward their car.

"Can we get out of here?" Eden said.

Johnny took Eden's hand in his and walked her to his truck. She said nothing on the ride home, so Johnny kept quiet, too. When they got inside, Eden collapsed on the couch. Johnny sat down next to her and held her. He was almost grateful she hadn't yet said anything, as he knew she was going to be pissed at him for hitting Todd. He was wrong.

"Thank you for sticking up for me," she said.

"I didn't want to interfere, but when I saw him getting ready to hit you, I couldn't let that happen."

"Nobody has ever defended me like that."

"You'll never have to worry about that again. I love you and I will protect you at all costs."

"Is your hand okay? I feel terrible that I'm just now asking."

"I'm fine. Please don't feel terrible after what you just went through."

She looked into his eyes, her heart overflowing with love for this incredible man. Running her fingers down his cheek, she leaned in and pressed her lips to his. She slid her tongue into his mouth. She felt Johnny's tongue dance with hers as their kiss deepened.

Eden stopped kissing him and said, "Dance with me, baby."

His mouth watering, Johnny stood and waited for Eden to turn on some music. She chose Kingdom Come's What Love Can Be. Johnny loved they shared the same taste in rock music. She walked over to him and threw her arms around his broad chest. He pulled her in close as their bodies started swaying together. She ran her hands up his chest, unbuttoning his shirt. He loved how her fingers felt running down his chest. She removed his shirt and tossed on the couch, then started showering his chest with soft kisses. He felt his dick stir.

"Fuck, angel," he said.

He lifted her shirt and removed it, along with her bra. He pulled her in close again, feeling the warmth of her naked breasts against his chest. And damn, it felt amazing. His large hands covered her back as they continued dancing. Eden bent back as Johnny ran a hand up her stomach to her breasts. He pulled her upright and sucked on each gorgeous breast, his tongue teasing her hard buds.

She lifted one leg, which Johnny grabbed and held up. He started grinding his pelvis against hers like one of her favorite scenes in Dirty Dancing. She matched his rhythm as they moved together until the song ended.

"I think we need to move this to the bedroom, sexy. I need to show you just how much I appreciate you coming to my defense today," she purred.

He watched her sexy hips sway as she sauntered into his bedroom. She pointed to the bed, so Johnny laid down. She unzipped his jeans, freeing his rock-hard erection. She slid his pants and underwear off, then removed his socks and shoes. She licked her lips as she ogled his naked body. He got up and stood behind her, sliding her jeans down. He hooked his thumbs under her panties and slid them down, then removed the rest of her clothes. They spent the rest of the afternoon in bed making love, then enjoying a nap. They woke up around dinnertime, both of them starving after their afternoon of passion. Eden was lying in Johnny's arms, her head on his chest.

"Any idea what you want for dinner?" Eden asked.

"I'd love to cook tonight, if you'd like to help me."

"I'd love to."

They were about to get out of bed when Eden's cell rang. She saw Hannah's name on her screen.

"Hey, Hannah, what's up?

"Wanted to first check on you after earlier."

"I'm fine. Thank you for asking."

"I'm so glad. I hate to ask you this, but could you do me a favor?"

"Sure."

"I'm ready to try talking to Johnny, but I'm nervous about calling him."

"I'm willing to ask for you, or I can let you talk to him on my phone."

"If you wouldn't mind, could you give him your phone?"

"Of course. Just a sec."

Eden smiled as she handed her phone to Johnny. She walked out to the living room, closing his bedroom door to give him some privacy. It elated her that Hannah wanted to talk. She knew that was weighing on Johnny's mind since he'd told Hannah his big news. He emerged from the bedroom a little while later, a big smile on his face.

"Change in plans for tonight, if you don't mind," Johnny announced.

"Of course I don't mind."

"Hannah invited us over for dinner. She asked me to ask you if you would mind taking Cocoa for a walk with Mikael after dinner so she and I can talk."

"I would love to. I'm so happy she's ready."

"Thank you, angel. I don't know what I'd do without your support."

"You're strong, you'd be just fine."

"Maybe, but I'm stronger with you."

"We're stronger together. I love you so much," she professed.

"I love you, my angel."

They grabbed a shower together, then got dressed to head over to Hannah and Mikael's house. Johnny was deep in thought on the ride over, so Eden kept quiet herself. There was a bit of awkwardness when they arrived, but by the time dinner was over, Johnny and Hannah seemed more comfortable around each other. Eden insisted on helping Hannah clean up, so the men waited in the living room. When they were done, Mikael grabbed Cocoa's leash and he and Eden headed out.

"I'm still a little in shock, so bear with me," Hannah said.

"Trust me, I understand," Johnny said.

"Could you tell me a little about what our dad was like? Mom always had plenty of negative stuff to say, but I'm sure that was bitterness on her part."

"Dad was great. He was so supportive of me, of what I wanted to do. I knew early on that I wanted to be a drummer, and he always encouraged me. He worked all his life, but he always found time to spend with me."

"What about your mom?"

"She was just as supportive as dad. They always made sure I felt loved. They were my rocks when I went through something pretty tragic and I'll never forget that. I'm curious. What was our birth mother like?"

Hannah's eyes filled with tears. "Nothing like your mom. She blamed me for our dad leaving and she never let me forget it. She's tall and model-thin and when I ended up looking like this, she berated me, always told me how ashamed of me she was."

Johnny put a hand on her arm. "I'm so sorry. I wish dad had taken both of us."

"So do I," she said. "You mentioned them helping you through a tragedy. What happened, if you don't mind sharing?"

"I got married in my early twenties. Two years into the marriage, Katie passed away from cancer. I never would have made it through that without them," Johnny said, tears in his eyes. "I swore I'd never give my heart to another woman. Then I found out about you and moved down here, and everything changed."

"I'm so sorry. And I can see what changed. The love between you and Eden is beautiful."

"I tried to fight it, but it was a losing battle."

"I get that. I tried like hell to resist Mikael. My head was full of all those insults mom would hurl at me and I had no self-confidence. Mikael changed all that, and I'll never stop being grateful."

Hannah stood and put her arms out. They were still embracing when Eden and Mikael got back. They stayed on the porch when they saw them.

"I'm so glad Hannah was ready to talk to him," Eden said.

"Me too. I didn't want to push her, but she needed to do it," Mikael replied.

"It was weighing on Johnny, but like you, he didn't want to push her."

"I'm happy he's had you for support."

Cocoa let out a loud bark, letting Hannah and Johnny know they'd returned. They walked out on to the porch, joining Eden and Mikael.

"Thank you both for giving Johnny and I the chance to talk," Hannah said.

"I second that. It was something we both needed," Johnny said.

"I'd like to continue building our relationship, if that's okay with you," she said to Johnny.

"Yes, and thank you both for having us for dinner tonight," Johnny said.

"It was our pleasure," Mikael said.

Eden walked over and gave Hannah a big hug, while Johnny and Mikael shook hands. They stood on the porch and watched as Eden and Johnny got in his truck. Mikael wrapped Hannah in his arms.

"Are you okay, baby?" Mikael asked.

"I'm getting there. Talking to Johnny helped, but there's still a lot I need to work through. I'm wondering if we should confront my mother," Hannah responded.

"Are you sure you want to put yourself through that?"

"No, I'm not. Johnny didn't mention it, so I'm not going to, but if he does, I'll at least consider it."

"We can discuss it more if it comes up."

"Okay."

Meanwhile, Johnny and Eden headed back to his house. He seemed to feel a little more relaxed than earlier.

"I'm glad you and Hannah talked," Eden said.

"Thanks, angel."

"What do you want to do tonight?"

"Would you mind if we just went home? I just need to hold you tonight," he said.

"I can't think of anywhere I'd rather be than wrapped in those strong, sexy arms, baby."

Once they got to Johnny's house, they changed into their pajamas and snuggled up on the couch. Johnny turned on a playlist of softer rock songs, which always helped him relax. Life had been such a whirlwind of late, between everything with Hannah and falling in love with Eden, and he needed to decompress. Johnny's couch featured recliners, so they were stretched out and comfy. Eden laid her head on his muscular chest and felt him sigh.

She looked up at him, gazing into his soulful eyes. He caressed her cheek as he crushed his lips to hers, his tongue teasing hers. She turned her body toward his, her closeness activating his launch sequence. She could feel his dick harden against her and moaned into his mouth as the heat built between her legs. They laid there kissing for a couple hours until Johnny fell asleep. Eden nestled herself and covered them in a blanket before drifting off herself. They awoke the next morning, still cuddled on the couch.

"How about a road trip?" Johnny asked.

"Where to?"

"Anywhere. Let's get in the car and drive."

"Don't you mean truck?"

"No, I have a surprise for you. Come to the garage with me."

Sitting inside Johnny's garage was a beautiful black 1973 Chevy Impala.

"When did you get this?"

"A couple of weeks ago."

"I love it Johnny. Let's go!!"

After having breakfast and showering, they got dressed and headed out. Johnny just started driving until they were on a deserted two-lane country road. There was nothing but open land as far as the eye could see, and no other vehicles anywhere to be found. The weather was perfect for driving, low 70s, a rarity for July in Pennsylvania, and sunny. The skies were a beautiful shade of blue, with nary a cloud to be seen.

Johnny stopped the car in the middle of the road, next to a field of wildflowers. He turned the music up full blast and got out of the car. Puzzled, Eden followed him. Johnny walked over to her and took her hand.

Def Leppard's Too Late for Love started playing. Johnny pulled Eden in close as they started moving to Joe Elliott's sexy voice. Eden straddled his leg as he dipped her back. She moved against him, getting his dick rock hard. He kissed her hard, his desire for her reaching the boiling point. When the song changed to Kingdom Come's Get it On, he pulled away from her so she could watch him dance. He ended his routine standing in front of the car, leaning back on the hood.

Eden walked over to him and put her hands on his chest. She unbuttoned and removed his shirt. She ran her hands all over his naked chest before moving down to his jeans. She unfastened them, smiling when she saw he was going commando. His dick sprung out of his jeans, ready and waiting for his sexy woman to play. She took his hand and led him into the field. She pointed at the ground, so Johnny laid down.

He kept his eyes on her as she removed her clothes in the most tantalizing striptease he'd ever seen. When his beautiful angel was naked, she straddled him, taking his dick deep inside her hot, wet pussy. She leaned back, using his muscular thighs for support as she fucked him, moaning with every journey her pussy made up and down his cock.

"Fuck, you're so damn good, angel," he said.

"Oh, Johnny, I love the way your cock fills me. Mmm, oh, so fuckin' incredible."

He loved the sweet torture of her slowed pace. This woman drove him wild in ways he never thought he'd experience again. He felt her body quiver as she approached the ultimate rapture. He felt her pussy tighten around him as waves of ecstasy rocked her body. She moaned as she exploded around him. Her moans were always the sweetest songs he'd ever heard, making his heart swell even bigger with the love he felt for her.

She moved off him and laid in the grass, spreading her legs wide. Johnny laid on top of her, using his hands to brace himself so his full weight wasn't on her. He slid inside her, filling her slick, wet pussy with his dick. Moving in and out of her while her nails raked his back was the most incredible feeling. Nothing was more incredible than being inside her, pleasuring her while his dick felt like it was inside a rain cloud.

"Mmm, angel, I love how it feels when I'm inside you. I love you."

"Oh, Johnny, I love you more than I've ever loved another human being."

She gazed into his eyes, hers smiling as much as her mouth was. He felt himself nearing orgasm and began thrusting harder. He watched her pleasuring her clit while he pounded her harder and harder until he filled her, groaning upon his release. He laid down next to her and pulled her close. The warm grass and wildflowers felt amazing against his skin, but not as amazing as the soft skin of the angel lying in his arms. After fucking a couple more times, they were starving. After getting dressed, they headed back toward home, and stopped at a little diner they found in a neighboring town.

Once they arrived back home, they spent the rest of the night cuddled up in bed, relaxing and watching TV until they both fell into a deep, restful sleep. The next morning, the sound of Johnny's cell phone awakened them.

"Hello," he said.

"It's Hannah. I hope I didn't wake you."

"Nope, I was up," he fibbed.

"I've been thinking about something since we talked and wanted to run it by you."

"Okay, what's up?"

"I want to talk to our mom about why she and Dad separated us when they split."

"Are you sure that's a good idea?"

"I want answers, but I didn't want to do anything until I talked to you first."

"What does Mikael think?"

"He's not sure it's the best idea, but he said he would support whatever decision I made."

"If it's okay, I think I'd like to talk with Eden first. Could I get back to you later today?"

"Of course. Thanks for listening, and I look forward to hearing from you."

"Goodbye," he said, then disconnected.

"What's going on?" Eden asked.

"Hannah's thinking about talking to our mother about why she let our father take me when they split."

"How do you feel about that?"

"I'm not sure, but while I am hesitant, I must admit that I'm also curious."

"I will support whatever decision you make. I just want you both to be 100% certain that's what you want to do before you do it. You may hear something you don't like, and once you do, there's no going back."

"Thanks, baby."

"You're welcome."

"I need some time to think about it, so I'll call Hannah back this afternoon. For now, how about we shower, then have some breakfast?"

"Sounds perfect."

After breakfast, they took a long walk around Johnny's neighborhood so he could clear his mind and decide what he wanted to do about Hannah's request. He still wasn't certain it was the best idea, but his curiosity won out, so he called Hannah after lunch and let her know that after giving it some thought, he wanted to go talk to their mother. Hannah let him know she would try to contact her and get back with him on when. Later that evening, she called to let him know their mom agreed to see them the following afternoon. Johnny was still a little unsure this was the best idea, and the ominous dream he had did little to allay his fears. He ended up having the worst night's sleep he'd had since he started seeing Eden. He would soon find out he should have trusted his instincts.

Chapter Eleven

Mikael and Hannah drove over to Johnny's house the following morning. Mikael waited back at Johnny's house with Eden. They were sitting in the kitchen having some coffee after Johnny and Hannah had headed out.

"I'm still not sure how good of an idea this is. I had the displeasure of witnessing their mother firsthand not long after meeting Hannah, and it was bad," Mikael said.

"I feel that same concern. I just keep hoping that with the two of them being together, it will make it a little easier."

"I hope you're right."

Johnny pulled up in front of their mother's house and turned off the engine.

"Not too late to change our mind," he said.

"I've done that about 100 times. Shall we head in before we chicken out?"

"I guess. United front?"

"Yes."

They got out of Johnny's truck and walked up to the front door. Hannah rang the doorbell and a few minutes later, they were face to face with their mother. She flashed a disapproving look at Hannah, but was stone faced when she looked at Johnny.

"Come in," she said, a coldness in her voice that gave Johnny the chills.

They followed her to the living room, where she motioned for them to sit down on the couch. Hannah and Johnny sat next to each, while she sat on the chair across from them.

"Well, I see you're still the same embarrassing pig, Hannah," she sniffed. "Did that man wise up and dump you?"

Her eyes filling with tears, Hannah responded, "We got married about a year ago."

"So, he's an even bigger idiot than I thought."

Johnny put a hand on Hannah's shoulder.

"And you," she said to Johnny, "are the spitting image of the piece-of-shit that was your father."

"Don't talk about him like that. You didn't even know him."

"I know he left me for that disgusting pig."

"She was an exceptional mother to me. Better than you would have been, from the way I see you treating my sister."

"Your sister is garbage. Tell me, are you seeing anyone?"

"I have a girlfriend that I love very much, something you're incapable of."

Her face, colored bright red, she stood and walked over to the couch, standing right in front of Johnny.

"I've been keeping tabs on you over the years, son. I know you lost your wife to cancer. I bet she made herself sick just to get away from you. Like your father before you, you'll never be anything more than shit. Do your girlfriend a favor, since like this one's husband, she's a moron for being with you, and let her go. Neither one of you jackasses deserves anything but misery, just like your father."

Hannah looked over at Johnny, but couldn't see any expression on his face. She wished she'd listened to Mikael and not done this. She wasn't sure what she thought would happen, but she should have known it wouldn't be pleasant. Digging down into the strength Mikael's love has given her. She stood straight, hands balled into fists and looked into her mother's cold eyes.

"You are a bitter old hag. You're the one who deserves to be alone. I hope you rot in hell," Hannah said before she stormed out, Johnny right behind her.

They walked out to his truck and headed back home. An awkward silence filled the truck, the tension so thick you could cut it with a knife. When they pulled into Johnny's driveway, she got out of the truck and was about to walk inside, desperate for Mikael's embrace, when she heard Johnny squeal back out of the driveway. Mikael and Eden raced out to the porch in time to see Hannah standing there, mouth wide open and see the back of Johnny's truck as he sped away.

"What happened?" Eden asked.

"Our mother knew everything about Johnny's life. She told him that Katie got sick to get away from him, and told him he would never be good enough for you, so he should let you go. That was after she finished berating me and telling me what an idiot Mikael was for marrying me. I'm so sorry, I should have listened to you," she said, looking at Mikael.

"I need to go after Johnny, but my car's at home. Could you drop me there?" Eden asked.

Mikael responded, "Can I give you some advice?"

"Okay."

"Don't chase him. He needs time. Trust me, as a man, I understand his reaction, and while he needs you, the last thing he wants right now is someone chasing him. I know the hardest thing for you to do is sit here and wait, but it's what you need to do."

"Okay, I trust you, Mikael," Eden said. "Now get Hannah home, as I'm sure she's also been through a lot today."

Eden went back inside after Hannah and Mikael left. She was worried about Johnny and was finding it hard to sit still, so she started pacing around his house. She was about ten minutes into her laps around his living room when she heard her cell phone ring. She saw Johnny's name when she looked at the screen and answered.

"Are you okay, baby?" Eden asked.

Ignoring her question, he said, "It's over."

"What's over?"

"This. Us. I can't be in this relationship anymore. My mother was right. You deserve better. Goodbye, Eden."

Before she could respond, Johnny disconnected. When Eden tried to call back, he didn't answer. She sat down on the couch, her body shaking, tears streaming down her face. She felt a pain sear through her heart like nothing she'd ever felt. She started feeling trapped, sitting here in Johnny's house, but she had no way to get home. It was too far for her to walk and she didn't want to bother Mikael and Hannah, so she dialed the number to her restaurant.

"Garden of Eden, this is Max. How can I help you?"

"It's Eden," she said.

"What's wrong?"

"Please come get me, I'm at Johnny's."

"Text me the address. I'm on my way."

Max left the restaurant in the hands of the night manager, and drove to the address Eden sent him. When she heard a knock on the door, she got up, praying it was Johnny. Why would he knock on his own door, stupid, she berated herself. Max took one look at her and pulled her into an embrace. He walked her over to the couch.

"Tell me what happened," he said.

"I don't know where to begin."

"Start from the beginning."

Eden filled Max in on everything, including Katie's death, finding out Hannah was his sister, and ending with the fiasco that was visiting their birth mother.

"I don't even know what to say, except I'm sorry," Max said.

"I just don't understand what I did to make him end things," Eden said.

"I know you won't believe me right now, but you did nothing."

"Then why? I don't get this at all."

"From everything I've observed, Johnny is strong and proud. He's most likely embarrassed at how he let his mother get to him. Instead of dealing with that, he lashed out at you. It's often the person we love the most that suffers when we're angry. He needs time. Promise me you'll be there for him when he's ready."

"I promise. But what if he's never ready? I can't even bear the thought of never seeing him again."

"I know it doesn't feel like it now, but he will come back. It's obvious to anyone with eyes how much he loves you. He just needs time to process everything that happened today. For tonight, though, do you want to stay here, or do you want me to drive you home?"

"Home, please. It's where I need to be right now to deal with this. It's too hard to stay here without him."

"I understand."

After Max dropped her off at home, she collapsed on her couch, a fresh wave of despair washing over her. She laid down on the couch and pulled a blanket over herself. She cried herself to sleep. The next several days were a blur. This was supposed to be a nice, relaxing week away from work with her man, and instead, it turned to heartbreak. Sunday afternoon, she drove to the dance studio, hoping that Johnny would at least show up for class, but he never did. She told Rebecca he was under the weather, so Derek stood in as her partner.

Though it was the last thing she wanted to do, Eden got up bright and early Monday morning and opened the restaurant. On the surface, she was her usual cheerful self, but Max could see a sadness in her eyes. He could only be there for her and pray that he was right about Johnny returning. About an hour after opening, Eden saw Mikael heading across the street.

"Good Morning, Mikael. Here to order some breakfast?"

"No. Johnny didn't come in this morning. Is he okay?"

"I don't know. I haven't seen him."

"Wait, what? He never came home that day?"

"No. He called me and broke up with me, and that's the last I heard from him."

"Oh, Eden, I'm so sorry. What are you going to do?"

"There's nothing I can do. I don't know where he is or where to even look for him."

"I could ask Hannah if anything he said to her would give us a clue, if you'd like."

"I appreciate the offer, but you two have enough to deal with."

"The offer stands if you change your mind."

"Thanks."

Feeling bad that he couldn't help her, he ordered two coffees and two danish to go then headed back across the street. Eden went about her day, trying her best to keep her focus on work and not on Johnny, but damn, she missed him. She was worried about him. She hated he was going through this alone. She wanted nothing more than to hold him. She was getting ready to head home for the day when she saw Hannah and Mikael come into the restaurant.

Hannah walked over and hugged Eden. "I'm so sorry. I feel like this is all my fault."

"Not at all. Johnny decided to go, but the only person I blame is your mother," Eden responded.

"I agree. I just wish I knew where we could start looking for Johnny," Hannah said.

"I might have an idea," Mikael said. "Give me a minute."

Mikael grabbed his phone and called Dean. After a few minutes, he walked back over and told them they'd have reinforcements. A little while later, Dean and his friend Chris came in. Chris was the local district attorney, and he could call in a favor and get the okay to check Johnny's cell phone activity. He told the judge Johnny was a potential threat to himself, so the judge agreed and signed off.

"The most recent location on Johnny's phone is Scranton," Chris announced.

"I bet I know where he is then, the cemetery where his parents are buried."

"Let's go," Hannah said.

"I appreciate the offer, but I won't chase him. Mikael and Max both told me I need to give him time, so I'll do just that."

"What if he needs you?"

"I don't want to push him and drive him further away. I love him and I want him back more than anything, but he needs to be ready first. Chris, I appreciate your help, as it makes me feel a little better knowing where he is."

"My pleasure," Chris said, then he and Dean headed out.

"Is there anything we can do for you?" Mikael asked.

"I'm okay. I'm just going to head home and try to keep my mind off things. Thank you, though."

They all walked out together. Eden felt a pang when she saw Mikael and Hannah leave together. She wished more than anything that she was going home to Johnny. She headed home, her house feeling lonelier that ever. She sat down on the couch, her eyes filling with tears as she thought about all the fun times she and Johnny shared. She ached for his touch, his kiss, his skin against hers. Like every night since he'd left, she went to bed and cried herself to sleep, wondering if this pain would ever go away.

The next several weeks were more of the same. Eden went to dance class every week, and every week, she had to rely on Derek to be her partner. The other students didn't ask her about Johnny, but she swore she could see the pity in their eyes when they looked at her. Rebecca approached her after their last class.

"I'm sorry that Johnny couldn't finish the class. Is everything okay?" Rebecca asked.

"It's not, but I'll get through it. Thanks for asking. I doubt I'll be completing in the showcase, though, unless I do it alone."

"I'm fine with that. You earned your chance to perform." She handed Eden a piece of paper. "Here's my cell phone number. Call me with your decision."

"Thank you. You're a great teacher, and I had fun."

"Take care, and I hope to see you next month."

Eden waved and headed home. She was hoping she and Johnny would do the rumba at the showcase, but she couldn't do that dance alone. She just hoped he was okay and finding the peace he needed to come back to her. She missed him so much, but she couldn't be mad at him, given what his mom said to him. She knew Hannah was also upset, but at least she had Mikael. Hannah debated about going to find him, but she was worried about how he might react, so she stayed put.

Meanwhile, Johnny was sitting in a hotel room in Scranton, feeling numb. He had spent each day since he got here at the cemetery, just talking to them. He told them about finding Hannah, about falling in love with his angel, and about the devastating words his birth mother had spit at him. He spent his nights in the room, aching to have Eden back in his arms. He loved and wanted her so much, but he knew he would never be the man she deserved. He almost dialed Eden's number a bunch of times, but he feared she would hate him, and he couldn't face that. He kept hoping his angel would come rescue him, but she was probably too hurt to bother.

He walked out to his truck and headed over to the cemetery. He sat down on the ground in front of the tombstone with his parents's names on it, tears filling his eyes. He wished more than anything they were still here. He knew they would never have made him feel like his birth mother had. He also wished they could have met Eden. If only they were still here and able to give him advice on what to do about her.

He couldn't get Eden off his mind, and he was going crazy. He knew he missed the rest of their dance classes, which made him feel even worse, since she was so excited when he got her that gift. He wondered if she was still going to do the showcase or even if she finished the classes without him. He knew he fucked up, but he didn't know how to fix it. Day after day, week after week, he kept coming to the grave every single day.

He was sitting there one Sunday afternoon, a week before the showcase. He laid down on the grass like he'd done on most of his visits and dozed off. This time, though, was different. His parents' voices jarred him from his sleep. How could he be hearing their voices if they had passed away?

He opened his eyes and came face to face with his parents. Confused, he couldn't speak, so he just laid there, staring at them. He could see the concern in their eyes as they watched him laying there, despair written all over his face.

"Hello, son," he heard his father say.

"Hi, Dad."

"Son, please don't take what the evil woman said to heart. Go back to your angel."

"I want to, but I can't. I broke her heart."

"Yes, you did, son, but it's not too late to fix it. We checked on her, and she is aching for you to come back into her life."

"Your father's right," his mom said. "She needs you, and you need her. Please. Go to her."

Johnny sat up with a start. He knew his parents were right. He couldn't stand even one more second without his angel. He stood up and said goodbye to them, then checked out of his hotel and started the drive back to Lancaster. The drive felt like it was taking forever, as all he could think about was seeing Eden. He wondered if she had stayed at his house all this time or went back home. Not seeing Eden was a disappointment. When he got into the living room, there was an envelope standing up in front of his TV.

Dear Johnny,

I'm so sorry I wasn't enough for you. I thought what we had was amazing, but I guess I was wrong. I'll always love you and I'll always cherish the time we had together. I hope someday you find the peace and happiness you're seeking.

Love, Eden

Johnny felt like someone had punched him in the gut. His beautiful angel thought she wasn't enough? He hated himself for how he made her feel. He knew he had to fix this, but how? That's when it hit him. He grabbed his cell phone and dialed. Once he got the information he needed, he got to work putting his plan into action. He drove over to Mikael and Hannah's first. Hannah opened the door and greeted him with a hug.

"Are you okay? Eden was so worried about you."

"I just needed some time. I went back to Scranton and spent every day talking to my parents. They came to me in a dream yesterday and told me to come back to Eden. Now I just need to convince her I'm hers for good this time. And that's why I'm here."

Johnny told Mikael and Hannah about his plan. They agreed to help. Mikael called Dean and filled him in, so he agreed that he and Alex would also help.

"Before I go, I just wanted to say how much I enjoyed working for you," Johnny said.

"What do you mean, enjoyed?" Mikael said.

"I figured I would no longer have a job after what happened."

"Under the circumstances, we can let this slide. I've experienced yours and Hannah's mother firsthand, so I get the havoc she can wreak."

"Are you sure?"

"We'll see you first thing Monday morning," Hannah said.

Johnny smiled and went back to his truck. He drove down to Garden of Eden and almost went in, but he wanted to wait until it was time to put his plan into action. Instead, he went to take care of the rest of what he needed to have his plan come to fruition. Once he was done, he went back home. Now he just had to sit tight until the weekend. He had to fight the temptation on more than one occasion to go see Eden, but he held out and Sunday morning rolled around.

Chapter Twelve

Johnny woke up, excited to put his plan into action and win his woman back. He knew they would have a lot to talk through, but first he needed to get her to at least be willing after the way he hurt her. He grabbed a quick breakfast, then showered and got dressed in his costume. When he was ready, he drove over to the dance studio. Rebecca let him know she would sneak him in through her entrance so Eden wouldn't see him. When he called Rebecca, she told him that Eden still wanted to be part of the showcase, so she was going to dance a solo. She would soon find out Johnny had something else in mind.

It was a few minutes before the scheduled start of the showcase. Johnny peeked out and saw that Hannah, Mikael, Dean, and Alex were all sitting in the front row. He quick darted back into Rebecca's office to make sure Eden didn't spot him. Rebecca told Johnny that Eden would close out the show, so Johnny sat and waited while all the other couples performed. When it came time for Eden's solo, Rebecca introduced her. That was Johnny's cue to get into position side stage.

Eden was expecting Heart's Alone to play. It broke Johnny's heart when he found out that's what she had chosen for her solo. Instead, however, the song Johnny and Eden planned use, Kingdom Come's

Perfect O, started. He heard Eden yell toward side stage that the wrong song was playing.

As he walked onto the stage, he said, "No, it isn't."

Eden's mouth dropped when she saw Johnny standing there. He was wearing loose cotton dress pants and shoes, but no shirt. He smiled when he saw Eden wearing the same outfit she had planned to wear for their rumba. He walked over to her and stood behind her, his hands on her hips. They started swaying to the music, as they had practiced. Not wanting to make a scene in front of the audience, she went with it. When he first moved in front of her, the look on her face was anger combined with hurt, but as they danced, he saw her face soften. Before long, the audience could see these two belonged together. The dance got sexier and sexier, leaving the audience hot and bothered. Their dance was by far the highlight of the night, met with a loud standing ovation when they were done, though Eden didn't hear it.

She ran off the stage as soon as the song was over. Johnny hurried off behind her, as Rebecca came out to close the show and thank everyone for attending. He was looking for her when he heard tires squealing. He looked outside and saw her tearing out of the parking lot. He turned to head back to the dressing area when he saw Hannah and Mikael, and Dean and Alex headed his way.

"Eden just took off out of the parking. I fucked up," Johnny said.

"She was probably surprised and didn't know how to react," Hannah said.

"Thank you for the kind words, but I have to face the fact that I just threw away the best thing that's ever happened to me. Why even bother going on without my angel?"

Johnny sank to the floor, his head in his hands. Alex walked over to him and sat down.

"I know we haven't met. I'm Alex."

"Hi."

"When I was in my twenties, I had an amazing boyfriend. His band got a record deal, and he left me to pursue his career," she said to Johnny, then looked up at Dean and mouthed sorry. "I was heartbroken and never let myself love another man. Then a couple of years ago, he came back into my life," she said as she pointed up at her husband.

"Don't give up just yet," Dean said. "Swallow your pride and admit you fucked up, but trust me, it will be worth it."

Johnny stood and put his hand out to help Alex up. She and Dean hugged him, followed by Hannah and Mikael.

"We're here for you," Hannah said.

"Yes we are," Mikael said.

"I can't thank all of you enough. I just don't know what to do. If she won't even give me a chance to talk, I'll get nowhere."

"Maybe something not as public when you try again," they heard a voice say.

The group turned and saw Rebecca standing there.

"Johnny, I'm so sorry. I thought, like you did, that Eden would love what you did. Give her a little time, then try talking to her again," Rebecca said.

"Thank you," Johnny said as he started heading out.

The rest of the group followed him, then got in their cars and headed home. Johnny wanted to go to her house, but he feared it was too soon after this afternoon's disaster. Instead, he drove over to the park and took a walk. Not long after he started his walk, he saw Eden. She walked past him, looking at the ground.

"Please, my angel, talk to me," he said.

"I'm not interested. You destroyed my heart and I'm just not ready to talk. In fact, I'm not sure I'll ever be ready," she said.

She didn't feel that way, but she couldn't let him know how desperately she wanted him back. She walked over to one of the picnic tables and sat down. He finished two laps around the park then, sat down on an empty bench. He turned his head when he heard someone cackling.

"I told you so. You're not good enough for her, loser."

Johnny looked over and saw his mother sitting on the next bench.

"Leave me alone. You've done enough damage," Johnny said.

"No, your asshole father did the damage. I just wish he'd left me before he impregnated me. Life would have been so much better if I hadn't had kids. I'm just glad blondie over there got smart. You're just like your father."

Johnny was about to respond when he felt a soft hand on his arm.

He looked up and saw his angel looking down at him. Eden turned her attention to the cranky old hag sitting on the next bench.

"You're right, he is just like his father. Your son is the kindest, most loving man I've ever known. While I never met your ex-husband, from everything Johnny's told me, he was a very special man. Too special for you. You should be ashamed of yourself for treating your children like this."

Johnny's mom opened her mouth to respond, but before she had a chance, Eden turned to Johnny and said, "Let's get out of here."

They walked out to the parking lot and walked over to Eden's car.

"Can we go somewhere and talk?" Johnny asked.

"Talk about what?"

"Us."

"There is no us. Look, I meant what I said back there. You are amazing, but I can't go through another heartbreak. I'm sorry."

Eden got in her car and sped out of the parking lot before she changed her mind. She loved Johnny more than anything or anyone, but if he hurt her again, she wasn't sure she would survive it, so she had to walk away. By the time she got home, she was fighting tears. She went inside and sat down on her couch, and the dam burst. Tears streamed down her face. She wanted nothing more than to get back in her car and drive to Johnny's house, but that would do nothing but make her feel worse. Instead, she had to figure out how the hell she was going to over him.

Johnny got in his truck and after a few minutes of sitting there, he pulled out and started driving. How was he ever going to get Eden to sit down and talk to him? He had so much he wanted to say to her, but wasn't sure he was ever going to get that chance. Before he realized what he was doing, he was pulling into Hannah and Mikael's driveway. Feeling stupid, he was about to back out of the driveway when Mikael walked outside and waved. He walked over to the truck.

"Hey man, what's up?"

"I was just at the park trying to clear my head and mom was there."

"Oh no. Why don't you come inside and tell us what happened?"

"Are you sure? I don't want to upset Hannah."

"I know my wife. She'll want to listen."

"Thank you."

They walked inside. Johnny saw Hannah sitting at the kitchen table. She looked up when she saw him and motioned for him to sit down. Mikael joined them.

"Your brother was just at the park and ran into your mom," Mikael updated Hannah.

Looking at Johnny, she asked, "What happened?"

"Eden was also there, and mom saw we were no longer together. She started on me again, this time berating me in front of Eden. Eden ended up coming over and defending me, but then she wouldn't go somewhere with me to talk. I can't take another second of not being with her, and I don't know what to do," Johnny despaired.

"How can we help?" Hannah asked.

"I just need to get her to agree to sit down with me, but she's so hurt. I never should have broken up with her."

"If there's one thing our mother's good at, it's wreaking havoc. She's so miserable that she wants everyone else to be that way. She tried with me, and almost succeeded, but then someone came into my life and changed all that," Hannah said, looking at Mikael.

"I had that someone and all I did was fuck it up."

"I need to tell you something, and I'm risking making myself look like a total dork," Mikael said.

"What?" Johnny asked.

"I screwed up and shared a picture of Hannah and I on social media without making it visible only to my friends. My ex-girlfriend saw it and sent Hannah a private message with some serious insults. Hannah was so upset that she took off. She hurt her ankle, so Alex and I went to help her and I dressed up in a superhero costume."

"You didn't look like a dork. It was sweet, and it helped me let you back in," Hannah said.

"You need to find your superhero move," Mikael said. "I chose an actual superhero since your sister loves them. Eden loves dance, so maybe that's what you need to do."

Johnny's face lit up.

"I just thought of something, but I need your help."

"Let's hear it," Hannah said.

Johnny filled Hannah and Mikael in on his idea.

"Oooh, Eden is going to love that," Hannah squealed.

"Thank you both for listening and for the help."

"Our pleasure. You two belong together, just like me and your sister."

Johnny hugged them both goodbye and headed out to his truck. Before he got on the road, he called Rebecca. After he explained what he needed, she agreed. He headed home to take care of the rest of the arrangements. If everything worked out, it would only be a few short days until he had his angel back in his arms. He headed off to bed early Sunday night, as he would head back to work on Monday morning. He was lucky that Hannah and Mikael let him keep his job. Hannah was waiting for him when he arrived in the morning.

"So, did you bring it?" Hannah asked.

Johnny handed her an envelope with Eden's name on it. She smiled and headed across the street to Garden of Eden. After ordering coffees and Danish for Mikael, Johnny. Kurt and herself, she handed the envelope to Eden.

"What's this?"

"No idea. I saw it tucked in the door, so I brought it in."

"Thank you."

"You're welcome."

"How's business? Everyone doing okay?"

"He misses you," Hannah said.

Eden didn't respond, for fear that Hannah would see right through her and tell Johnny she missed him, too.

"Your order will be ready in a few minutes."

Hannah nodded, but said nothing else. She just had to hope that Johnny's plan worked. She hated seeing her brother and Eden so down, especially when all they both needed was each other. Eden brought her order out and handed it to her.

"Thanks for stopping in."

"You're welcome."

Eden went back to her office to open the envelope. She wondered who was sending her something with such fancy handwriting. She took out the card that was inside, also written in the same fancy writing.

Masquerade Party

The honor of your presence is requested this coming Saturday at 7 PM.

The party will be held in the studio where our class was held.

Join your classmates as we celebrate a successful ballroom class.

Dress is formal and should include a masquerade style mask.

Eden wasn't sure she was up for going, but she enjoyed the class and didn't want to insult Rebecca and Derek by skipping it. A night out might do me some good, she thought to herself. She planned on wearing the light blue dress and heels she wore to the first class. She only wished everything was still the same as that class. She couldn't help but wonder if Rebecca invited Johnny and if so, would he be there. She pushed that out of her head and decided just to enjoy herself.

Hannah got back to her store and handed out breakfast. Once she got to the record store, she handed Johnny a coffee and Danish.

"I gave her the invite. She didn't open it while I was there, so I'm not sure what she's planning to do."

"I can't thank you enough for your help. I'm going to the studio Saturday morning to set everything up."

"Do you want some help?"

"I appreciate the offer, but you've done enough."

"Nonsense. It would be my pleasure. I'll recruit some extra hands and we'll get you set up in plenty of time to get home and get ready."

"This means the world to me. I can't take much more of the pain of not having that woman. I'm in love with her and I want to spend the rest of my life with her. I never thought I would say that after I lost Katie, but Eden saved me. I have to fix this."

Grabbing his hand, tears in her eyes, Hannah said, "You will. I promise."

The rest of the week dragged by, even though they were busy. Johnny could think about nothing but Saturday. He was a nervous wreck. He didn't know how Eden would react when she realized it would just be the two of them. Saturday morning rolled around, and Johnny's nerves were at an all-time high. He got up early and loaded his truck with everything he needed to make tonight perfect for his angel. He pulled into the parking lot behind the dance studio and couldn't believe his eyes. Standing there waiting to help him were Mikael, Hannah, Dean, and Alex.

"I can't believe you're all here," Johnny said.

"We've all been where you are, longing to get the love of our life back in our arms," Dean said, looking at Alex.

The group followed him over to his truck and helped him unload everything. Once they got everything inside, the women took charge of how to set things up. Johnny appreciated having a female perspective so that everything would be perfect for Eden. The men took care of all the physical work and once they were done, the results amazed Johnny.

"Thank you all so much. All that's left now is hoping Eden shows up and isn't upset when she finds out it's just the two of us."

"We were more than happy to help. Now, get home and get ready to sweep that woman off her feet," Hannah said.

Johnny got home and took a nap so he would be well-rested for what he hoped was an eventful night. When he woke up, he grabbed a shower and got dressed. He grabbed his mask and headed back down to the studio to get everything turned on and ready before Eden arrived. He stood at the window, watching for her car. His heart started beating out of his chest when he saw her pull in. He sent a quick text to Hannah to let her know Eden showed up. She texted back a smiling face and a heart. He turned his phone off so nothing would disturb them. He left the studio so she wouldn't see him until he was ready to surprise her.

Eden entered the studio and couldn't believe her eyes. Where is everyone? She started looking around, her eyes wide. Bouquets of sunflowers lined the entire perimeter of the room. There was a beautiful king-sized canopy bed in the middle of the room. She also saw a table for two, complete with a cheese and cracker tray. There was a bottle of wine and two glasses on the table. The room went dark, causing Eden to gasp. The lights turned back on and...

Chapter Thirteen

. . . Eden was standing face to face with a masked man. He pulled a remote control out of his pocket and she heard Still Loving You by Scorpions play. He walked over to her and knelt before her, taking her hand in his.

"May I have the honor of this dance?"

"You may."

Johnny took her into his arms and pulled her in close. She wrapped her arms around him as they swayed together to one of the most romantic rock songs ever. She knew they still had plenty to talk about, but for right now, she was going to enjoy being back in her man's arms. She inhaled, his sexy cologne driving her wild. They gazed into each other's eyes as they danced, lost in each other. When the song ended, Johnny walked her over to the couch.

"What's going on? I thought I was coming to a party for our ballroom class."

"I'm sorry for misleading you, but I needed to get you alone so we could talk. I have so much I need to say. I love you, Eden."

"Then why the hell did you dump me? You shattered my heart into a thousand pieces."

"I know and I can't tell you enough how sorry I am. What my

mother said rattled me. She told me I wasn't good enough for you and I believed her. I can't believe I let her get in my head like that."

Eden took Johnny's hands in hers.

"You could have talked to me. I could have helped you," she said.

"I know. I was so distraught at what my birth mother said that I wasn't thinking straight. I know that's no excuse, but it's the truth. I went back to Scranton and spent every day at the cemetery talking to my parents. The Friday before the showcase, they came to me in a dream and told me to come back to you. I was so afraid you'd refuse to see me, so I concocted the plan to surprise you at the showcase, and Rebecca was kind enough to help me. But that was the wrong direction to take. I realized that what I needed was to be alone with you."

Her face softening, she said, "I had fun when we danced at the showcase but then seeing you afterward brought everything rushing back."

Johnny said, "I had fun too, but I realized it was too much for you to deal with in front of so many people. I love you so much and I don't want to spend one more night without you in my arms. Please, baby, I'm so sorry. Please give me another chance."

Eden could see the sincerity in his eyes. Without another word, she threw her arms around his neck and crushed her lips to his, jamming her tongue into his mouth. He pulled her in tight, returning her kiss, their bodies wrapped around each other as they kissed.

"Baby, I want you, right here, right now. Please, baby, I need to be inside you, to make love to you. We have the studio all to ourselves until tomorrow morning."

"Oh, Johnny, take me, please, baby. I've missed you so much."

Johnny stood and helped her up. He unzipped her dress and let it fall to the floor. His heart started racing when he saw her standing there in light blue lingerie and heels. She was the most exquisite woman he'd ever seen and he couldn't wait to spend the rest of the night showing her just how much he loved her. She unbuttoned his shirt and dropped it on top of her dress. After removing his belt, she unfastened his pants and let them fall to his ankles. He stepped out of them, then kicked off his shoes. She looked down and let out a little giggle at the sight of him standing there in just underwear and socks. He joined her with laughter as he removed his socks. He removed his underwear, then sat down on the couch.

She stood in front of him, licking her lips as her eyes drank him in. She removed her bra and panties and was about to remove her shoes when Johnny stopped her.

"Please, my angel, leave those sexy heels on."

"Mmm, naughty man."

He wagged his finger at Eden, so she walked over and sat on his lap, taking the full length of his dick inside her. She slid up and down as they fucked hard, achieving climax. She pressed her heaving chest to his as he held her tight.

"Oh, angel, I missed feeling you. I promise I'll never hurt you again."

"I missed you too. Please, baby, next time, just talk to me. I love you and I'm always here for you. Now, please take me to bed. I want to spend the rest of the day naked with you."

Johnny scooped his naked angel into his arms and carried her to the bed he set up in the middle of the studio. He laid her down, then joined her. He pulled her close and kissed her with more passion than she'd ever felt. Eden ran her fingers through his hair as they kissed. He ran his hands down her back to her soft, sexy ass. She moaned into his mouth as her hands explored his sexy chest. Her hands continued its journey down his body. He groaned when she took his dick in her hand and started stroking his erection.

He laid his lover on her back and licked the entire length of her neck, sucking as he went. She knew she was going to have hickeys, but at that moment, she didn't care. He trailed his tongue between her beautiful breasts, then sucked them one at a time, his tongue flicking her hard nipples. He heard her emit those quiet moans he loved so much. Eden writhed beneath him as he worked his magic on her breasts. She grabbed his ass, squeezing hard, as he showered her stomach with tender kisses. He was getting closer to her pussy, and she wanted him so badly, she was aching.

He ran his tongue all over her belly, causing her to shiver with pleasure. He slid his tongue down her abdomen. He teased her by skipping the part she most wanted him to touch and ran his tongue down her thighs. He started sucking on the insides of her legs until she couldn't take it anymore.

"Please, baby, my pussy is throbbing for you."

"In due time, my love. I want to pleasure you from head to toe."

"Oh, Johnny."

He moved down to her feet, kissing the tops of each foot, then running his tongue up the length of each of her sexy legs. He moved back to her abdomen, stomach, and breasts, continuing to avoid her pussy.

"Please. I can't take another second of this. Please, Johnny, I need your fingers, your tongue, your dick, anything on my pussy now."

Johnny flashed her a wicked smile as he trailed his tongue back down her abdomen. This time, he stopped between her legs, burying his tongue in her wet folds. He swiped his tongue up and down her pussy, caressing her clit. She emitted more of those soft moans he loved so much.

"Mmm, so good, Johnny."

He kept up his soft, slow pace as she moved beneath him. He gave her clit a couple hard sucks, then returned to his light licks, as she ground against him, her release building so slowly that it was driving her out of her mind.

"Baby, please go harder," she said.

He flashed her a look that got her way closer to her orgasm, but he ignored her request. He slid his tongue deeper into her pussy, still licking up and down. He inserted a couple of fingers and slid them in and out of her. He felt her body shiver as she moved closer and closer to climax. He could feel how close she was, so he started sucking hard on her clit until she came undone.

"Oh, Johnny, so fucking good, don't stop!"

Jolts of electricity rocked her body off the bed as she emitted loud moans. Johnny kept sucking her clit, causing her to come again and again, each time more powerful than the one before, until she was screaming so loud they probably heard her in the next town. He stopped sucking her clit and instead stroked her g-spot with his strong fingers. He increased the pressure until he felt warm liquid drench his hand as her body convulsed in an orgasm so powerful she let loose the sexiest combination of dirty words he's ever heard.

"Oh, Johnny, that was so damn fucking incredible! I love the way you sucked the hell out of clit, then fucked me so hard with your sexy fingers that my pussy exploded all over you. Holy fuckin' shit, baby. Now get on that sexy back of yours so I can wrap my mouth around that hard cock while you spank my ass."

"Oh, fuck, my beautiful angel. Get on those knees and suck me, woman."

She opened her mouth wide and slid her lips and tongue up and down his shift as she squeezed his balls. She moaned when she felt one hand connect with her ass and the other massaging her tits. She teased his cock, sliding her mouth up and down. She removed her mouth from his dick and sucked on his balls as he growled with pleasure. She felt him nearing orgasm, so she returned her mouth to his dick, this time sucking hard and fast.

"Oh fuck, woman, so fucking good."

He emptied himself into her mouth. Gazing into his eyes, she swallowed every delicious drop, then licked her lips. She was so fucking hot. He loved the sight of her on all fours, sexy heels on her beautiful feet, her ass pink from his hand. He wanted nothing more at that moment than to have his dick deep inside her.

"On your back, and spread those sexy legs, angel," he said.

"Mmm, Johnny."

She laid on her back and spread her legs wide. He eyed her up and down, never tiring of the sight of her naked body. He got off the bed and grabbed a wedge. She lifted her ass so he could slide it underneath her, angling her body so he could get deep inside her. She moaned when he slid the full length of his dick into her pussy. She locked her legs around his waist and planted her hands on his ass, trying to pull him in even deeper.

He rocked her pussy with slow, deep, powerful thrusts, groaning each time he moved inside her. Damn, he'd missed this. Nothing had ever felt quite like making love to this beautiful woman. She felt so damn good wrapped around him. Each thrust was hitting her g-spot hard. He felt her tremble, so he started pounding her harder and faster until they exploded together, her pussy drenching his dick as he filled her with his seed. Johnny laid on his back next to her. She rolled toward him, resting her head on his broad chest, her long blonde hair tickling his naked skin.

"I love makeup sex," she purred. She ran her tongue over his nipple, sending shivers down his spine.

"Oh, yes, angel. Thank you for being willing to hear me out."

"My pleasure," she said, flashing him that wicked smile he loved so much.

"Mine too, baby."

She ran her fingers down his chest and abs, then traced that sexy 'v' that pointed to her favorite part of his body. Her touch excited him, and he was hard again. Eden looked up at him and batted her lashes while she licked her lips. She straddled him and pressed her chest to his, kissing him hard, her tongue intertwining with his. He loved the way her skin felt against his. She ran her tongue down his broad neck, tracing his sexy tattoo with her fingers.

"Fuck, you look so good on top of me, my angel."

She smiled, then resumed her sexy tongue bath. She teased each of his nipples, then slid her tongue down his chest to his abs. She ran her tongue along each side of his v. She was so close to his dick, he could feel her warm breath, and he wanted more. He wanted to fuck that pretty mouth again.

"Baby, I wanna feel those hot lips around my dick."

She turned her body around so he had a full view of her hot little ass. She lowered her head and took him into her mouth. He loved the sound her mouth made when she sucked his dick.

"I'm such a naughty girl sucking on your hard cock, and I need to be punished," she purred.

As she returned her mouth to his dick, she felt his hand connect with her ass. She was so turned on, her pussy was dripping. While spanking her with one hand, he slid the fingers of his other hand between her legs and stroked her clit. She started rocking her body, and he felt like he was going to explode.

"Fuck, you're so damn hot, woman. Nobody has ever sucked my dick quite like you and it feels so damn good. I love watching that sexy ass and those sexy tits bouncing. Now, get that pussy on my cock."

She kept her back to him and took him inside, leaning back, using his chest to support herself. Damn, she loved how he filled her. She slid up and down his cock. His firm hands held her hips as she shattered around him. He fucked her hard until his cock emptied inside her.

"I never want to experience another night without you in my arms," he said.

"I've missed you so much, my sexy man. We have so much sex to catch up, but first, I'm famished. Can we have some wine and cheese?"

"Wait here, beautiful."

Johnny walked over to the small table as Eden's eyes followed his sexy naked body. He returned with two glasses of wine and the cheese tray. They sat on the bed and polished off their wine and the entire cheese tray. Johnny carried everything back to the table, then put his hand out. She stood up and joined him as he turned more music on.

"Come dance with me, my angel."

She always enjoyed dancing with her man, but there was something primal about doing it naked. Her body was on fire from head to toe as she swayed in his arms. He leaned his head down and kissed her hard. She could feel him getting hard again.

"Oh my, someone's ready to play again," she said.

"It's because you're so fucking hot, woman. My dick wants nothing else but to be inside your hot pussy. Get on your knees on the couch, baby."

She knelt on the couch, holding on to the back for support. She felt Johnny behind her, spreading her legs and fingering her slick pussy. He grabbed his dick and plunged it into her sweet pussy as his hands found her sexy breasts. He moved one hand to her hip, stroking her clit with the other while they fucked. The sound of his body slapping against her sexy little ass was so fuckin' hot.

"Oh, Johnny, that feels so fuckin' good. I wanna taste your cream, baby. Please fuck my mouth."

"Come back to the bed with me, baby."

Johnny laid down and watched his sexy angel crawl across the bed.

"Now, get those sexy lips around my dick while I suck your hot pussy."

She straddled his head, then took his dick into her mouth. She gasped when she felt his fingers spread her folds as he buried his tongue into her honey. He sucked her clit hard while he watched her beautiful head bob up and down, her lips and tongue making his dick feel so good. She stopped at the head and started twirling her tongue around, teasing him. That earned her a swat on her ass, so she kept teasing him.

He spanked her a few more times until her sexy ass was pink. He nipped and sucked at her clit, feeling her tremble. She moaned, the vibration setting his cock on fire. He stroked her g-spot with his fingers until she exploded, her love raining down all over his face and chest. That was so fucking hot that he exploded himself, filling her pretty mouth with his salty goodness. He loved watching her swallow him, never wasting even one little drop. They laid together, both of them spent from hours of incredible passion.

Looking up at Johnny, Eden said, "Thank you for tonight. This was incredible."

"Baby, I love you so much and I can't tell you enough how sorry I am for breaking your heart."

"I love you too. Trust me, after seeing your mother in action, I understand. She seems good at getting under your skin."

"I'm kicking myself for letting her, but after everything I've been through, I let her get in my head. From now on, I will follow my heart, a heart that is filled with more love for you than I could ever hope to express with words."

"Believe me, you don't need words. The way you made my feel tonight, not to mention all the other times we've made love, there is no doubt in my mind how much you love me."

"I don't know about you, my angel, but I'm spent. How about we get some sleep?"

Eden yawned and said, "I'm exhausted, but damn, it was worth it!"

Johnny turned out all the lights, then rejoined his beautiful woman in bed. He pulled the covers up and pulled her close. She fell into a deep sleep in his arms. He kissed the top of her head, then joined her in dreamland. Johnny's cell phone awakened them in the morning.

Hannah was calling to see if he was ready for the crew to help him clean up. He let them know he was, but didn't tell anyone that Eden would be there.

They got dressed and started packing things up while waiting for the others to arrive. Hannah squealed with joy when she came in and saw Eden standing there. She ran over and gave her a big hug. Everyone realized when they looked at the bed that Johnny and Eden made up over and over. Every time Johnny passed her, he touched her, earning amused looks from the rest of the group.

Once they had everything packed up, they loaded up Johnny's truck. Everyone congratulated them on making up. Hannah mentioned making plans for a group outing soon. The other couples headed home, leaving Eden and Johnny in the parking lot.

"Baby, will you come home with me?"

"Of course. I just need to stop home and grab some stuff. I took everything home after, well, I need to grab some clothes and toiletries."

"Okay, baby. Do you want to get some breakfast first?"

"Dressed like we are?"

"Why not? Let's hit the diner."

"What the hell!"

Heads turned as they walked into the diner, dressed to the nines. They sat down at their favorite table in the back. They placed their order and waited for some coffee. Johnny took Eden's hands in his, as they gazed into each other's eyes. He took a deep breath, a nervous look on his face.

"I've been thinking about something and I wanted to run it by you," he said.

"Okay."

Chapter Fourteen

"I want us to live together."

"Oh my god, Johnny, are you sure?"

"Yes, baby. I don't want to wake up another morning without you."

"I would love to."

"You just made me the happiest man in the world."

"Can we go out tonight and celebrate? I'd love to go to the club."

"Yes, my love."

They finished breakfast, then paid the check and headed out. Johnny followed Eden to her house to help her grab some of her stuff. They ended up taking most of her clothes and enough toiletries to last until she could pack up more. He helped her carry her stuff out to her car. They drove over to his house and carried her stuff inside. Johnny had an empty dresser in his bedroom, so Eden unpacked her clothes. She couldn't contain herself. She walked over to Johnny and threw her arms around his neck, crushing her lips to his.

"What was that for, angel?"

"For this. I love you so much and I'm so happy to be here."

"I love you and I can't wait to wake up every morning gazing at your beautiful face."

"I can't believe how much my life has changed since I met you. I was so sad and lonely, and then this strong, silent, sexy drummer danced his way into my life and stole my heart."

"I'm just sorry I broke that heart."

"That's behind us. We had a minor bump in the road on our journey, but we found our way back to each other and that's what matters. Together, we can overcome anything."

Johnny pulled her in tight. He never tired of feeling this incredible woman in his arms. Eden wrapped her arms around him, stroking his strong back with her hands before moving them to his ass and squeezing hard.

"You are so damn naughty, woman."

"Because you are so damn sexy and I can't keep my hands off you."

He scooped her up in his arms and carried her to the bed. Clothes flew everywhere as they pawed at each other. They spent the afternoon in bed making love until they were both unable to move. After a nice long nap, they showered together and got ready to head out to the club. They were just about to head out when Johnny's phone rang.

"Hey, Mikael, what's up?"

'One sec, let me check. "

"How would you like to make tonight a group outing?" he asked Eden.

She nodded yes.

"That sounds great. What time?"

"Okay, see you then."

"We're meeting Mikael, Hannah, Dean, and Alex at the club tonight at 7."

"Okay. That sounds like fun. Are we going to tell them about me moving in? I'm fine either way, just didn't want to say anything wrong."

"You could never say anything wrong, but thank you for checking. And yes, I want the world to know!"

"Me too," she said.

"Speaking of you moving in, when do you want to pack the rest of your stuff?"

"I was thinking I might do a little each night after work on the nights I don't have to close, then more on the weekends until I move everything in."

"That sounds great. We can take my truck to work everyday so we have more room to load boxes."

"But I start earlier than you."

"And? I can help you open, then head across the street. The more time I get to spend with my angel, the better. I'm looking forward to tonight."

"Me too. I'm so glad you and Hannah are getting closer."

"Do you think you'll see your family again?"

"I doubt it. They blame me for everything that's happened. I think I'm better off without them. You're my family now."

"Oh, baby," he cooed, then kissed her. "Wait until I get you back home tonight."

"Back to our home. It feels so good to say that. I never felt like Todd's house was ours, just that he let me live there so I could plan his parties."

"You'll never have to feel that way again. I have a thought, though. How tied to your house are you?"

"It's just the first thing I bought after leaving Todd, so it doesn't have any kind of special place in my heart."

"And mine, I am renting as, like you, I just needed to find a place to live when I moved here. Maybe we should look for something to purchase together."

"A new beginning, something that's just ours. It sounds perfect! I paid for my house out of the settlement Todd's dad gave me, so I can sell and we have that money to use."

"Are you sure? You could invest that back into the restaurant instead."

"I'm sure. I want to do this."

"Thank you. Shall we head out?"

"Yes, my love, let's go dance the night away!"

They pulled into the club parking lot and saw Hannah and Mikael walking in. Johnny called out to them, so they waited and the two couples walked into the club together. Dean and Alex were already sitting at a table right down front. The group walked over and sat down. A few minutes later, a waiter stopped by and took their drink order while they looked over the menu.

"Does everyone want a meal, or just order a bunch of appetizers we can all share?" Dean asked.

Everyone else agreed to appetizers, so when the waiter brought their drinks, Dean gave them the food order and asked for six plates. They all enjoyed their drinks while they waited for their food.

"Don't forget, we need to keep an eye on these two," Mikael said to Dean, pointing at their wives.

"Why's that?" Eden asked.

"We were here last Halloween. Hannah and I had a bit too much to drink and we're told we put on a quite a show on the dance floor," Alex admitted.

"We, of course, have no memory of it," Hannah said.

Everyone laughed as their husbands teased Alex and Hannah for their spectacle.

"I may not even dance tonight, with this talented beauty," Hannah said, pointing at Eden.

"I'm nothing special," Eden said.

"I beg to differ, my love," Johnny said. "In fact, we had been planning to come out tonight even before Mikael called. We have something pretty major to celebrate."

"Do tell," Mikael said.

"This beautiful woman agreed to move in with me. We decided that we're going to buy our own place together. It will be a brand new beginning for both of us."

Hannah looked at Eden and saw her grinning from ear to ear. Everyone congratulated them and when their second round of drinks came, Mikael toasted their reunion and wished them well on their house hunting. After they finished their food, Alex and Hannah were getting antsy to hit the dance floor.

"Eden, would you like to join us?" Hannah asked.

"Why not," she said.

All eyes were on them as the three of them danced together. Johnny couldn't help but stare at Eden. Her beautiful blonde hair was bouncing along with her body, as Johnny felt his dick stirring in his pants. Fuck, she was so damn sexy. Hannah and Alex interrupted his daydream by running over to the table. They grabbed Johnny and pulled him to where they were just dancing. The amused looks on their faces caused Dean and Mikael to join them.

The music changed and Eden held her hand out to Johnny. He took her into his arms and they treated the rest of the crowd to the sexiest damn dance anyone had ever seen. Mikael and Dean grabbed their wives and joined them. Everyone was watching Eden and Johnny. They looked so good together. Their ballroom lessons had paid off, and they almost looked like professional dancers.

A couple of slow songs followed, so all three couples remained on the floor. The guys all held their woman close, looks of bliss on all their faces, as they were with the three hottest women in the room. Eden had never been one for female friends, but Alex and Hannah had changed that, and she found she enjoyed hanging out with them. More than anything, though, she loved seeing Johnny so happy. He had been through so much tragedy in his life that he deserved this happiness. Eden had her share of heartbreak, but she hadn't had to experience the same level of tragedy as her man had.

Johnny whispered something in Eden's ear, causing her cheeks to flush. They rushed off the dance floor and headed for the bathroom area. They found an empty dressing room in the hall and snuck in. He looked at the door behind him and pulled her in tight, jamming his tongue into her mouth as he crushed his lips to hers.

"Baby, all that dancing woke my dick up. I couldn't wait one more second to bury myself inside that sweet pussy."

"Oh god, Johnny, I'm so wet. Please come fuck me."

He took her jeans and panties off in about five seconds flat. He smiled as she laid down on the couch and spread her legs wide. Her pussy was glistening, and he couldn't wait to get his cock inside her warmth. He removed his pants and underwear.

"Baby, if you don't get that cock inside me, I'm going to explode. I want you so fuckin' bad."

"Damn, woman," he said as he lowered himself on top of her and slid his massive dick deep inside his sexy woman. They fucked hard and fast, both of them so turned on from dancing together, that they couldn't come fast enough. They both exploded hard, trying to stifle their screams as Johnny filled her while her body quaked hard from an earth-shattering orgasm. They dressed and casually walked back to the table. Their flushed faces gave away what they had just done.

Johnny saw Alex and Hannah lean over and whisper something to Eden, the three of them bursting out laughing. The guys, meanwhile, were busy giving Johnny high fives. He looked so happy to have a couple of male friends, just as she was finding out how much she enjoyed the company of Hannah and Alex. Part of her was fearful at how wonderful everything was going. She feared something was going to happen that took everything away from her. She pushed all that aside and went back to enjoying her night out.

They stayed until the club closed. They all walked out together, laughing and joking. Everybody hugged goodbye, then each couple headed home. Johnny headed toward the park and pulled into the parking lot.

"What are we doing here at this hour?"

"I thought we could take a walk before we head home."

"The park closes at dusk."

"Come on, baby, be a rebel."

"I'm thinking you're a bad influence on me," she said.

"Don't even try that. That bad girl has always been inside you."

"What the hell, let's do it."

They held hands and walked back to the pond. They sat down next to each other on the dock. Johnny pulled her in close and kissed her. She threw her arms around him, twisting her tongue around his. He laid her back, never breaking the kiss. He slid his hands under her shirt and opened her bra. His hands squeezed her beautiful breasts as their kissing intensified. His touch had her pussy soaking wet as a moan escaped her lips.

He lifted her shirt and lowered his mouth onto her breasts, sucking them as his tongue flicked each nipple. Her body writhes beneath him, desperate to feel his touch between her thighs. She felt him unfasten her jeans and lifted her bottom so he could strip her naked. He removed her shoes and socks, then finished removing the rest of her clothes. The full moon was casting beautiful light on her sexy body. He loved watching her lying there naked. She spread her legs wide, giving him a full view of her sweet pussy.

"Mmm, my angel, your body looks even sexier under the moonlight."

"Then get those pants off and get that dick inside me. I wanna fuck."

He stood up and removed his pants, then sat back down.

"Baby, please come sit in my lap."

She lowered herself into his lap, wrapping her pussy around him. He wrapped his arms around her as she bounced up and down on his cock. There was something so primal about fucking outside like this that had her even hornier than she usually was.

"Oh, Johnny, it feels so good. I love you."

"Baby, I love you too," he said as she felt him shoot his load inside her.

She bounced harder and faster as she neared climax. She cried out like a wolf howling at the moon, her body convulsing as she shattered around him. He pulled her tight against his chest, both of them breathing hard and fast, covered in sweat and other fluids.

"I think we need to cool off," he said.

Before she could respond, she felt him pick her up and next thing she knew, she was in the cool lake. He joined her, pulling her close as the water splashed around them. She splashed him, then swam away. He followed her, catching her and pulling her in tight. She wrapped her legs around his waist. He felt her hand stroking his dick under the water, and he was hard again. She grabbed his dick and slid it into her pussy. They fucked hard, this time in the water, both of them coming again. After a couple laps, they got out and just laid on the dock. After their skin dried a bit, they got dressed and raced out of the park before they got caught.

They got home and got ready for bed. They were both exhausted from their night out at the club and their little tryst in the park. Eden was about to put on her sleepwear when Johnny stopped her.

"You don't need that," he said.

"Oh, and why not?" she said.

"I love feeling your naked body next to mine when we sleep."

"Oh, Johnny."

They got into bed and Johnny pulled her in close. She fell asleep nestled in her lover's arms. He loved the sound of her soft snores as she slumbered next to him. He fell asleep, still holding her. Something poking her awakened her the next morning. Johnny was still asleep, but his dick sure wasn't. He was sporting full-on morning wood. She took her hand and stroked his erection, causing him to stir.

"My, my, you're insatiable, my love."

"It's not my fault. Your snake woke me up, so I thought he wanted to play."

"Oh, baby, he always wants to play inside that sweet pussy. Get that sexy body on top of me. I want you so fucking bad."

After a quick, hard fuck, they showered and got ready for work. Johnny parked behind Hannah's store, then he and Eden walked across to her restaurant. He helped her get everything ready for the busy morning rush. When it was time for his shift to start, he kissed her goodbye and walked back to the record store. The morning was slow, but lunch finally arrived. He, of course, went to Garden of Eden to eat. Max made Eden take a break and enjoy lunch with him. She sent him back with a bag of brownies for his co-workers.

When he finished for the day, he came back to Eden's restaurant and helped her get ready to head home. They were just walking over to this car when they saw Mikael and Hannah come out. Hannah ran over and gave Eden a big hug.

"We need to have you two over for dinner and a game night some time." Hannah said.

"We'd love to," Eden said.

"I'll talk to Alex and maybe we can do something this weekend."

"Sounds great."

Eden and Johnny spent every night after work packing up more of her stuff. They left what she didn't need at the house, so they didn't have to move it twice. Once they finished that, they planned to attend open houses. In the meantime, they searched real estate websites in their free time.

Chapter Fifteen

The weekend rolled around, and Eden was excited. They spent the morning doing more packing and then headed home to get ready for dinner and a game night at Mikael and Hannah's. Dean and Alex would also join them, and they already decided it would be a competition between the men and the women.

They had all agreed on making it a potluck, so Eden was in the kitchen getting her contribution, dessert, ready. She was making her favorite, Death by Chocolate. She knew she couldn't go wrong with chocolate and Kahlua! Of course, she and Johnny also had to make sure they fit a quick fuck in before they got ready to go. She found it impossible to keep her hands off that sexy man.

They pulled into the driveway right after Dean and Alex, so both couples walked in together. Dean and Johnny joined Mikael in the living room while the women stayed in the kitchen to help Hannah get everything ready to serve. Eden and Alex helped her carry everything to the dining room table. The men joined them, everyone sitting down to indulge in delicious food and wine. Eden's dessert was also a big hit. The men insisted on cleaning up since the women did all the cooking. Once they were done, they got the table set up for game night.

They started with Pictionary. The women were in sync and kicked the men's asses. The guys kept teasing them about cheating, but in the end they all admitted that their women were the brains of the operation. They joked and laughed throughout the entire game, especially when the woman drawing barely drew anything and the other two would guess it right away. The men challenged them to a best two out of three, which, of course, the women won. After they were done, the six of them went into the living room to just sit and talk. Loud talking and raucous laughter filled the room until they heard a cell phone ring.

"That's mine," Eden announced. "I'll be right back."

A puzzled look appeared on her face when she saw the caller ID.

"Hello."

"This is Eden Mitchell."

"What can I do for you, officer?"

"I don't understand."

Her face crumpled and her phone fell from her hand. Johnny raced over and caught her just as her knees buckled. He walked her over to the couch and sat her down, then tried to hand her phone to her, but she refused.

"I apologize sir, Miss Mitchell dropped her phone."

"I'm her boyfriend. Let me ask her."

"Can he fill me in? You just need to say yes into the phone," Johnny said to Eden.

"Yes, officer."

"What? Oh no. What do you need us to do?"

"Okay, thank you."

Johnny put her phone down and pulled her into a tight embrace, stroking her hair as she sobbed into his chest. The rest of the group watched with concerned looks on their faces.

"Can I tell them?" he asked Eden.

Unable to speak, she just nodded yes. Johnny motioned the rest of the group over so he didn't have to shout across the room. The other couples came over and joined them. Johnny took a deep breath, dreading having to say this out loud. He wished he didn't know what Eden was going through, but he'd been there, and he knew she was hurting. He took another deep breath, determined to get through this without breaking down himself.

"That was a police officer calling to give Eden some devastating news. Her parents, her sister and her ex-husband were leaving an event when a drunk driver struck their vehicle. I wish I didn't have to say this, but there were no survivors."

Everyone gathered around Eden, holding her, as tears spilled from their eyes. Nobody knew what to say, as nothing at that point would make her feel better, so they all just held her. She held onto Johnny for dear life and she couldn't bring herself to lift her head from his chest. She didn't know what to say, what to do, anything, so she just sat there and buried herself in her man. After a little while, she lifted her head and looked at everyone.

"I'm so sorry for ruining everyone's evening," Eden said.

"Oh, sweetie, you ruined nothing. I'm so sorry about what happened. I know words can't provide much comfort right now, but please know I'm here if you need anything," Hannah said.

"We all are, Eden," Alex said.

"Thank you. I hope nobody thinks it rude, but I need to go home."

"We understand," Mikael said, as Dean nodded in agreement.

Eden tried to stand, but found her legs wouldn't support her and she fell back on the couch. Hannah held her until Johnny stood and scooped her up in his arms. He carried her out to his truck and got her into her seat, then went back inside to get her things. Hannah put Eden's phone into her purse and handed it to Johnny, then gave him a hug.

"Please let us know if there's anything we can do," Hannah said to Johnny.

"Give Eden our love," Alex said.

They all hugged Johnny and walked him out to his truck. They all stood on the porch huddled together as they watched Johnny back out of the driveway and head home. They walked back inside and helped Hannah clean up. They all sat down on the couch, still in shock at what had happened.

"Poor Eden," Alex said.

"This also has to be hard on Johnny, bringing back a lot of painful memories. Even though the circumstances differ, the loss isn't. Johnny was married when he was younger and lost his wife to cancer. More recently, he lost his mother, the one who raised him, and our father," Hannah said to Alex and Dean.

"I didn't know he'd been through that much tragedy himself. Is that how he found out about you?" Alex asked.

"Yes, his father left a letter with his attorney to be given to Johnny when our dad passed. That letter told him about my existence. He moved here to find me and ended up also falling in love with Eden."

"I don't know what to say. Will you let me know if you plan on doing anything for her?" Alex asked.

"Of course, I'm thinking I might make some food to take over."

"I will as well. Let's talk tomorrow and decide what."

"Sounds good."

Dean and Alex headed home, leaving Mikael and Hannah just standing there, numb. Mikael held his wife in his arms. She pulled away and went into the kitchen to clean up, her eyes filling with tears.

"Baby, this can wait until morning. Right now, I just want to go to bed and hold each other," Mikael said.

Hannah fell into his arms, so he walked her to the bedroom and helped her get ready. They collapsed into bed and fell asleep, holding each other tight.

Meanwhile, Johnny pulled into his driveway. He walked around to the passenger and helped Eden out. She could walk this time, but Johnny still held on to her, just in case. They walked inside and Eden sat down on the couch, her head in her hands. She didn't say a word on the ride home, just sat and stared out the window. He was struggling to find the right words, if there was a such thing in a situation like this. He walked over and sat down next to her, wrapping her in his arms.

"When you're ready to talk, I'm here, my angel," Johnny said.

"I don't know what to say, what to do, even what to feel right now," Eden said.

"I understand. I felt the same way when I lost Katie and my parents. I was just lost."

"I'm sorry. I shouldn't be going on about my problems, after what you've been through."

"Don't say that, baby. I'm here for you and I will help you through this. I don't care what time of day or night it is. Even if you need to wake me, I will listen."

"Oh, Johnny," was all that came out before her body started shaking.

She sobbed into his chest like she had earlier. Johnny felt his heart breaking in two as he held her. They sat like that for over an hour until he felt her lift her head.

"Thank you for being here. I don't know what I would've done if I'd been alone when I got the phone call."

"I love you and I will always be here for you, baby."

"I love you. Can you do me a huge favor?"

"Anything."

"Can you call Max and tell him what happened? I'm still going to work on Monday, but I just want him to know ahead of time."

"Okay to calling him, but please, baby, take some time off work."

"I can't. The restaurant needs me."

"Baby, right now, YOU need you. Please, just think about it."

She nodded as she watched Johnny dial Max's number. When Max answered, Johnny filled him on what happened. Max asked to talk to Eden, so Johnny handed her the phone.

"Thanks, Max."

"No, I'll be in first thing Monday morning."

"I can't. That's too much to put on you."

"Fine, but only for a week."

"Thank you, Max."

She put the phone down and looked at Johnny. "I'm going to take a week off. Max told me as much as I need, but I think a week will be plenty."

"Okay, but if at the end of the week, you feel you need more, don't be afraid to take it."

"Thanks. Would you mind if we went to bed?"

"Of course not."

"I just need to be in your arms tonight."

He helped her up from the couch and held her hand as they walked to the bedroom. They climbed into bed and Eden nestled herself against her man. He pulled the covers up and pulled her in tight. She fell asleep on his chest. He kissed her forehead, then fell asleep himself. Her voice awakened him in the middle of the night.

"I'm sorry for waking you."

"Not at all. I told you any hour, day or night, I'm here."

"What do I do now? You've been through this."

"Are you sure you want to do this now?"

"I need to, please."

"Okay. We're first going to need to know what their wishes were. I think our best bet is to get a lawyer or talk to their lawyer. Did they ever discuss anything about their will with you?"

"No, because I left. I know who their lawyer is."

"Okay, then I think we need to start by calling them on Monday morning. What we do next will depend on what they tell you."

"Thank you. I know this is a lot to ask, but will you go with me if they want to talk to me in person?"

"I will go with you anywhere you need me to. You will not have to do this alone."

"Thank you."

She kissed him on the lips, then laid on her side and fell back asleep. He spooned her and draped an arm over her. This time, she slept through the rest of the night, awakened from her slumber by the scent of coffee and bacon. She padded out to the kitchen, where Johnny was finishing cooking breakfast. He poured her a cup of coffee and walked it to where she sat. She gave him a weak smile and took a sip of the coffee. He brought two plates of food over when he finished cooking and watched as she picked at her food.

"I know I need to eat, and I'm trying."

"I know, angel."

She finished her plate. When she tried to help Johnny clean up, he wouldn't let her. Instead, he talked her into grabbing a shower and getting dressed. She came out a little while later in a t-shirt and jeans. They were sitting on the couch when they heard a knock at the door. Johnny opened the door and saw Mikael and Hannah and Dean and Alex standing there holding bags. Eden got up and joined them.

"Hey everyone. I'm sorry again about last night," Eden said.

"And as we said, you have nothing to apologize for. How are you feeling this morning?" Hannah asked.

"Still numb," she said.

"I can only imagine, sweetie," Hannah said as she and Alex started unpacking their bags.

Eden watched in disbelief as they unpacked several casseroles, salads, and desserts. There was more food than she and Johnny could even think about eating. They were just finishing unpacking when there was another knock at the door. This time it was Max with a ton of food his mother made.

"I can't believe you all did this. I can't tell you how grateful I am. I would love it if you would all have dinner with us tonight," Eden said.

"Are you sure you want that many people here?" Alex asked.

"I do. I consider all of you friends, and it would help to have you all here."

They all agreed to come back over around dinnertime. Eden thanked them again for all the food. When everyone left, she walked over and wrapped her arms around Johnny.

"Thank you again for being here. Would you mind taking me to the park? I feel like I need a break from being inside."

"Of course, let's go."

Johnny took her hand as they walked around the trail. They got back to the lake and took a seat on the dock. Eden smiled a little. Johnny looked at her with a puzzled look on his face.

"I was thinking about the other night. I know it's not the most appropriate thing to be thinking about, but it's helping keep my mind off everything else."

"I know what you mean. I looked for anything I could to distract myself."

Johnny put his arm around her. She laid his head on her shoulder as they sat and watched the water rippling with the light breeze that was blowing. Eden jumped a little when her cell rang. She saw her parents's lawyer on her caller ID. She answered, putting the phone on speaker.

"Hello."

"May I please speak with Eden Mitchell?"

"This is she."

"Miss Mitchell, this is Larry Paul, your father's attorney. I apologize for calling on a Sunday. First, let me say that I'm sorry for your loss."

"Thank you, sir."

"I would like to set up an appointment for us to speak. Are you available tomorrow?"

"I'm taking some time off work, so yes, I can come in. What time?"

"Does one work for you?"

"Yes, that will be fine."

"I wish it were better circumstances, but I look forward to speaking with you tomorrow."

"Thank you, Mr. Paul."

Eden disconnected and put her phone away. She couldn't help but wonder what we would have to tell her tomorrow, but for tonight, she just wanted to focus on having their friends over for dinner. She still couldn't get over their generosity, making all that food for her.

"Can I ask you something?" she said to Johnny.

"Anything, sweetheart."

"How am I supposed to be feeling right now?"

"Baby, only you can answer that. You tell me."

"I'm not sure. I'm not happy this happened, despite how they treated me, but I'm also not feeling that devastation that I imagine you felt."

"With the different way our parents treated each of us, I don't think anyone would fault you for how you feel."

"Thank you. I'm so lucky you're in my life."

"We're both lucky. I know it doesn't feel like that now, but it's true."

"One more question."

"Of course."

"Does it make me a horrible person that I want to go home and be intimate?"

"Not at all."

"Then could we go home? I feel a little awkward saying this, but I just want to lie together and make love. I just feel like I need to be as close to you as I can. I hope it makes sense."

"It does, my angel. Let's go home."

They drove home, then went inside and walked into the bedroom.

This differed from the other times they'd been together. There was no dirty talk, just two people who loved each other and needed each other. They both removed their clothes and laid down together. Johnny laid on top of her, bracing himself with his hands. Eden wrapped her arms around him as he lowered his head and kissed her. He and made love to her. They held each other when they were done. She felt a bit of healing. She was with a man who loved and respected her enough to give her what she needed.

"Thank you, Johnny," she said.

"I love you."

They grabbed a quick shower, then got dressed and waited for their friends to arrive. Eden knew she had a lot of tough days ahead of her. She still didn't know what her father's lawyer would say, but she knew with the help of Johnny and her friends, she could get through anything. The three couples had a quiet evening of good food and good company, what Eden needed. Once everyone had gone home, she and Johnny headed to bed.

Chapter Sixteen

Eden woke up early the next morning. Unable to fall back to sleep, she got out of bed and walked out to the kitchen to get the coffee started. Her nerves were getting the best of her, anticipating what she would hear from Mr. Paul this afternoon. She had this deep fear that her parents left something scathing in response to her leaving. She heard Johnny stirring. He walked up behind her and wrapped his arms around her.

"Good Morning, my beautiful angel."

"Mmm, good morning, Mr. Sexy."

She poured two cups of coffee and put them on the table.

"What would you like for breakfast?" Eden asked.

"You!"

"Oh, Johnny. Seriously, though."

"I would love some pancakes. I'm happy to make them if you're not up for it."

"Thanks, but I would love to cook."

"Okay. I'll go grab my griddle."

"Oooh, dirty," Eden said.

That was met with an eye-roll followed by a laugh as Johnny went to the pantry to get his griddle. Eden got the ingredients she needed and put the pancake batter together while the griddle warmed up. Once she finished cooking, they sat down to eat. She loved sitting across the table from him while they ate. She needed him now more than ever and reached her hand across the table, grabbing his. He gave her hand a light squeeze, making a smile appear on her beautiful face.

"Anything you want to talk about, angel?"

"I'm dreading this afternoon. I keep imagining all these bad scenarios, like a scathing letter or something else to hurt me because I left."

"I understand. I didn't know what to expect when my dad's lawyer wanted to see me. All I can say is try not to think the worst. I know that's easier said than done."

"It is, and that's why I'm so grateful that you'll be with me."

"Are you sure you want me to go into the meeting with you? I'm happy to wait in the lobby if you prefer."

"Thank you, but yes, I want you in there, especially if it's something upsetting."

"I'll be by your side, always."

"Once we clean up, can we take a soak in the tub before we have to get ready to go?"

"It would be my pleasure, angel."

"I love you, Johnny."

"I love you too, Eden."

They cleaned up after breakfast. Johnny poured them each another cup of coffee to drink while they relaxed in his tub. She always felt better in the warm water with all the jets surrounding her body. Of course, the best part was sitting there naked with her sexy man. After a long, relaxing soak, they took a hot, steamy shower together, then got ready for their meeting. They pulled into the parking lot at the law firm a little before one.

"Are you ready, angel?"

"Yes, baby. Let's get this over with."

They walked inside and approached the reception desk.

"May I help you?"

"My name is Eden Mitchell. I have an appointment with Mr. Paul."

"He's expecting you. Right this way."

They followed the receptionist down to his office. Though the door was open, she still knocked.

"Miss Mitchell has arrived for her appointment."

"Thank you, Jane. Miss Mitchell, please come in and have a seat."

"Thank you. This is my boyfriend, Johnny. I hope it's okay that I asked him to join me."

"Of course. Have a seat, please."

Johnny sat down in the chair next to Eden.

"Let me again tell you how sorry I am, Miss Mitchell."

"Thank you."

Mr. Paul picked up an envelope off his desk and handed it to Eden.

"Before you open that, let me give you a little background," he said.

"Of course."

"Your father entrusted me with this document to be given to his next of kin in the event of his passing. Given the circumstances, that became you. I'm going to step out and give you some privacy while you peruse the document."

"Thank you, sir."

He nodded, then walked out of his office, closing the door behind him. Eden opened the envelope and removed the papers inside. She hesitated to open them, however, as she didn't know what she was about to read. Eden opened up the document and started reading. When she was done, she looked up at him, unable to speak after what she just read. She handed the paper to Johnny. Johnny read through, his jaw dropping.

"I can't believe what I just read," she said.

"Me either. What does this mean? For you, for us?"

"The only thing I can tell you right now is that it changes nothing for us, relationship-wise."

Johnny sighed and grabbed her hand. A few minutes later, Mr. Paul re-entered his office. He could tell by the looks on Johnny and Eden's faces they had both read the document.

"Do you have questions, Miss Mitchell?"

"I need to make sure I understand this correctly. Everything goes to me. The company, the house, all of their assets?"

"Yes, that's correct."

"What happens if, for example, I decide I don't want the company?"

"That would depend on what you mean. If you outright don't want the company, we would look for a buyer. If, however, you want to keep the company but be a silent partner, we would leave you as owner and find a new CEO. I don't expect you to have an answer today. I'm sure this is a lot to take in, so please take some time to think about things."

"What about the house? Do I have the option to sell if I decide? I'm not saying I will, as like you said, I need time to digest all of this, but trying to get an idea of my options."

"Yes, ownership will transfer to you as the sole heir, then it will be up to you to decide what to do. I will also be on your retainer to help you along the way, something else your father setup."

"Thank you. Could we schedule another meeting for a week from today? That will give me time to talk about everything with Johnny and decide what I want to do?"

"Yes, of course. I'll have my receptionist schedule something. Is there anything else you wish to ask me today?"

"No, sir."

"That's your copy of the document, so take that with you."

"Thank you for your time, Mr. Paul."

"You're welcome. I'll see you in a week. If you have questions in the meantime, please give me a call."

"I will."

They all stood and Mr. Paul walked them out to the reception area.

"Jane, please schedule an appointment with Miss Mitchell for one week from today."

"Yes, sir."

After her appointment was scheduled, Eden and Johnny walked out and got in his truck. They just sat there, both of them still in shock at what they just learned.

"I'm a millionaire." Eden said. "My brain can't even process that. For now, I want to keep this to ourselves. I'm worried about people coming out of the woodwork if they find out."

"You have my word, baby."

"What I still don't know is what I need to do regarding funeral plans. I hate to say it, but I think I'm going to need to contact Todd's parents. I know they will take care of Todd's arrangements. What I'm not sure about is Morgan."

"I'll be there for whatever you need, including running interference if you need."

"Thank you. I will want you with me, but I need to face this."

"That's my angel."

"Right now, I just want to go home and spend a quiet evening together."

"I can't think of anything I'd rather do."

The best laid plans, she thought to herself when they pulled into the driveway and saw a Lincoln Town Car. She knew that car anywhere and tensed up. Johnny looked over when he heard her sigh.

"Let me guess, Todd's parents?"

"Yes. I knew I would need to see them. I just hoped it would be on my terms."

"I'm right here with you."

"Thank you."

They got out of Johnny's truck, and she wished she was surprised they'd found her, but she knew deep pockets could get anything they wanted. As she approached their car, Todd's parents, Richard and Emily, got out.

"Good Afternoon, Eden," Emily sniffed.

"Hello. I'm so sorry about Todd."

"Like hell," Emily snorted.

"Emily," Richard warned. "Thank you, Eden. We've come today to discuss funeral arrangements, if that's okay."

"Of course. Would you like to come inside?"

"Please."

Johnny unlocked the door and stepped aside to allow Todd's parents and Eden to enter. He squeezed her hand as she went by. Emily looked around at the living room, then eyed Johnny.

"This is what you left my son for, you harlot," Emily said.

"Emily! Enough!" Richard scalded.

Emily sat down with a scowl on her face.

"We plan on having a joint service for Todd and Morgan, unless you would prefer to handle Morgan's," Richard said.

"I'm fine with theirs being done together since they were married. I'm also fine with handling my parents's services," Eden said.

"I should hope so, since you did nothing else but hurt them," Emily chimed in.

"I will not warn you again. We came here for a civil discussion, so please keep your commentary to yourself," Richard said to his wife.

She folded her arms across her chest, but didn't utter another word. Johnny couldn't help but notice that Richard never apologized to Eden for Emily's insults, but he kept that to himself. Eden had a deep frown on her face and the last thing he wanted was to make it worse.

"That will be fine. We will handle the obituaries for Todd and Morgan as well. We will list you as Morgan's sister, unless you prefer we don't."

"No, it's okay, as I'll be listing both Morgan and I in the ones for my parents."

"Very well. Should you choose to pay your respects at the service, we promise we'll be civil."

"Thank you. I will offer the same courtesy to you."

Emily opened her mouth, but a stern look from Richard changed her mind. He nodded to his wife, and she rose from the chair she was occupying.

"We must get going. Thank you again for being willing to talk with us. Would you like us to contact you when the final arrangements are made?"

"Thank you for the offer, but I'll watch for the obituary."

"Fine. We'll do the same."

Without so much as a goodbye, they turned and walked out the door, got into their car, and backed out of the driveway. Johnny closed the door. He walked over to the couch and sat down next to Eden. She laid her head on his shoulder. He felt something dripping on his arm. He turned Eden's head and saw tears spilling over. He embraced her tight as she cried into his shoulder.

"I'm so sorry Emily was so rude to you," Johnny said.

"I deserved it. I left her son."

"You did not deserve it. I will refrain from any additional comments under the circumstances, but you were justified."

"I can't thank you enough for being here for me."

"No need to thank me. How about we get started on our quiet night?"

"Yes, please. Could we do pizza and Netflix marathon? I need to PIV-OT my mood," she said.

"Friends it is, angel."

He kissed her, then called to order dinner. While they waited, they changed into their pajamas. Once the pizza arrived, they set themselves up on the couch and spent the rest of the evening enjoying dinner and laughing at the antics of her favorite TV characters, Phoebe and Joey, a much needed stress-reliever. Eden knew things wouldn't ease up as tomorrow she would need to visit her parents's church to make the arrangements for their service. Then she still had to face both services. She dreaded having to face so many people from her past, most of whom held her in disdain since the real reason her marriage failed was kept secret. For tonight, though, her focus would remain on Johnny and the love he'd brought to her life.

The next morning, they headed down to Garden of Eden to grab breakfast and so Eden could check on things. Her staff all rushed over and hugged her when she walked in. Max let her know everything was fine when he brought them their breakfast. After they ate, they drove to her old hometown and pulled into the parking lot at Fisher & Sons Funeral Home. The owner, Nathaniel Fisher, greeted them when they walked in. He took them to his office.

"I'm so very sorry for your loss, Miss Mitchell. Your parents were pillars of our small community."

"Thank you."

"This won't take long at all. Your parents were very specific about they wanted. They also provided their obituaries, so I'll just need your approval."

Nathaniel pulled a file out of this drawer and went through everything with Eden. She approved everything, so all that was left was to talk cost.

"What do I owe you for everything?" Eden inquired.

"That's also already been taken care of. Your parents left us more than enough to cover everything, so we owe you a refund."

"I would prefer to leave that with you as a gratuity for the clergy, if you would be so kind."

"Yes, of course, we will take care of that for you. Given the amount, however, the clergy will only accept a portion. May we provide the rest as a donation to the church?"

"Please, and could that be done in the names of my parents, my sister, and my brother-in-law?"

"Yes ma'am."

"Thank you."

Once Eden signed all the required paperwork, she and Johnny returned home. She was feeling restless and quite horny. She walked up to Johnny and grabbed his ass, squeezing hard.

"Angel," he said.

"I need to take my mind off everything and I need your help," she purred.

"Anything you want, baby."

"Please take me to bed, and fuck me harder and dirtier than you've ever fucked anyone."

"Holy shit, woman."

He picked her up and threw her over his shoulder. He carried her into the bedroom, put her down, and ripped her clothes off.

"How dirty to you want it?"

"As dirty as possible. I want one night where I can just forget about everything else going on right now."

"I promise you won't be disappointed. Get your hot little ass on that bed. NOW!"

She crawled onto the bed and laid down. She watched Johnny open the top drawer in his dresser. Her eyes went wide when he pulled out a set of restraints. He fastened her wrists to the headboard then put the ankle restraints on her, leaving her lying there spread eagle, her pussy wide open. He grabbed a set of feathers, a bottle of lube, and a rabbit-style vibrator from the drawer, then walked over to the bed.

For now, he left his clothes on, other than his socks and shoes. He dragged the feathers down her naked body, giving her chills from head to toe. He leaned over and sucked her sexy tits, biting her hard nipples.

He started teasing her pussy with the feathers as she moaned and writhed against her restraints.

"Tell me how that feels, baby."

"Mmm, so good, but I need more."

"Patience, my love," he said.

He took his fingers and spread her folds, running his tongue up and down her sweet pussy. He never tired of tasting her honey, and fuck she was wet. He stopped as quickly as he started and grabbed the vibrator. After applying lube, he turned it on full speed and slid it inside her while the rabbit ears vibrated against her clit. The vibrations were so intense, she screamed as she came undone. He left the vibrator where it was, the curvature stimulating her g-spot until she squirted hard.

"OH. FUCK. JOHNNY."

He watched with delight as she came hard several more times, her screams louder than anything he'd ever heard. He removed the vibrator and ran his fingers along her clit. Her pussy was so sensitive from her many orgasms that even the lightest touch was driving her wild.

"When do I get to see you naked?"

"When you've earned it."

"What do I have to do?"

"I need more motivation."

He walked across the room at sat down. She ached for his touch, but he wouldn't come near her unless she convinced him to.

"Baby, you just made me feel better than I've ever felt in my life. I've never come that hard before. Now I want to return the favor. I want to feel you fuck my mouth so I can drink you."

"I'm going to need more than that, woman."

"After I swallow you, I want to feel your cock come all over my tits."

"You're getting closer, but I'm afraid I'm still not convinced."

"When you're done soaking my tits with your hot cum, I want you to uncuff me so I can get on my hands and knees."

"Then what?"

"Then I want you to fuck my pussy like the dirty dog you are while you spank my naked ass."

"Oh fuck, woman."

He stood up and removed his clothes. He watched her lick her lips as more and more of his skin appeared. He removed his underwear, freeing his huge erection.

"Please let me taste that cock."

He straddled her, then grabbed his dick and entered her eager mouth. She slid her sexy lips and tongue up and down his cock, sucking him hard. Damn, this woman knew what she was doing. She felt him quake as he was close to exploding. She started sucking harder until he emptied down her throat. She swallowed every drop, then ran her tongue on the head so she didn't waste any of his salty goodness.

Looking at her laying like this, her eyes refusing to leave his body, he was hard again. He put his dick between her sexy tits, pushing them together with his hands. He fucked her sexy chest hard and fast, shooting another load, this time drenching her hot tits.

"Oh fuck, angel. Or should I say devil? You're so fucking hot. Look what you're doing to my cock."

She lifted her head and saw that he was hard yet again. He removed her wrist and ankle restraints and watched as she got on all fours in the middle of the bed. He knelt behind her and slid his dick inside her soaking wet pussy. He fucked her hard and fast, his hand connecting with her ass as his balls slapped against her with each hard thrust.

"Fuck, I love the way your massive cock feels inside me," she screamed.

"Nothing feels more incredible than being inside your hot pussy. Baby, I'm about to fill you. Please, baby, let's come together."

"Oh, Johnny," she said, as her body convulsed with the most intense pleasure he'd made her feel yet.

She felt him empty inside her as she came undone around him, both of them moaning, screaming, and growling like wild animals. They both collapsed on the bed, chests heaving, bodies drenched in sweat among other delicious fluids.

When she caught her breath, Eden looked over at Johnny and purred, "That's what I needed. Holy shit, my sexy stud, I've never done or felt anything quite like that."

"Baby, that was by far the most incredible sex I've ever experienced. You're a goddess, my angel."

She looked at their bodies, then looked at the bed and giggled.

"I think we have some cleanup to do," she said.

They got into the shower and cleaned each other, then changed out the bedding. Eden put the sheets in the washer and started the load. They grabbed a quick snack while they were waiting. As soon as she had the sheets in the dryer, they headed off to bed. Eden laid facing Johnny, as they gazed into each other's eyes.

"I love you so much, my sexy protector. I'm going to need a lot from you over the coming days. If at any point it gets to be too much, please tell me."

"Angel, I've been through this and I know how hard things are going to get. You will have my full support, along with that of our friends. We will get through this together."

They kissed, then drifted off to sleep, still holding each other. Neither of them stirred until the following morning.

Chapter Seventeen

Eden and Johnny spent the next several days preparing for the funeral service for her parents, which would be on Friday. Before that, though, she had to get through the service for Todd and Morgan, planned for Wednesday. Eden needed something to wear for the services, so Hannah and Alex took her shopping.

Eden didn't bring Johnny with her to her sister's service, as she didn't want to throw having a new man in the face of her ex-in-laws, so Hannah and Alex went with her for support. It was tough seeing her sister and Todd like that. They may not have treated her well, but she never wished them any harm. They stayed for the service after the viewing, but didn't do the cemetery or the luncheon. She just wanted this week to be over, but she had to stay focused, as there was still a lot to do. She didn't know what she would have done without Johnny and their friends.

For her parents's service, she talked to Max about holding the funeral luncheon there. He reached out to a couple of his friends who were also chefs, and they agreed to help him with the cooking. The day before, Dean and Mikael helped Johnny setup extra chairs and tables under a tent outside as they were expecting many mourners. She made a mental note that she was going to do something special for all of them, to thank them for all the support they'd given her.

Friday morning rolled around. Eden woke up and stretched, stirring Johnny out of his slumber. He pulled her close and kissed her forehead.

"Are you ready for today, angel?"

"As ready as I can be."

"Just remember, I will be right by your side."

"I love you."

"I love you too."

They had a quick breakfast, then showered and dressed. A limo would pick them up at 8 to take them to the funeral home. The viewing will be from 9 to 11, followed by a service, then the luncheon at Garden of Eden. They sat down in the living room while they waited.

"Can I talk to you for a minute? I've been keeping something in and I can't any longer," Eden asked.

"Anything, baby."

"I haven't seen or talked to my parents since I left Todd. Today will be the first time I'll be seeing them and it's like this. I'm feeling a lot of guilt."

"I understand, but remember, baby, they didn't give you a choice. Yes, you could have stayed and done what they wanted, but that wasn't living. You have a beautiful soul that deserves to be free. Had you stayed, that would not have been possible. So, today, you go there and make your peace with them, knowing that you did what you needed to do."

She threw her arms around Johnny and held him tight. They stayed in their embrace until they heard the limo pull up outside. Johnny stood and helped her up. They walked outside and got into the limo. A little while later, they pulled up at the funeral home. Nathaniel was waiting in the lobby to take them into the room where her parents were resting.

"Do you want to go in alone?" Johnny asked.

"No, I need you with me," Eden said.

Nathaniel opened the door. Johnny took her hand, and they walked into the room. As they reached the caskets, Eden's legs gave out, and she collapsed against Johnny. He held onto her as they stood in front of the caskets. Eden wept as Johnny held onto her. He felt his heart breaking seeing his angel so upset.

"Mom and Dad, I know you were always disappointed in me and my choices, but I had to be me. I'm sorry that I left, but you gave me no choice. I will always love you, but I will never regret doing what I needed to do."

Eden walked over to sit down. Nathaniel walked over to Johnny and let him know the doors would open to the public in about 15 minutes, in case Eden wanted time to compose herself. She walked to the restroom to wipe her face and returned a few minutes later. She walked over to Johnny and wrapped her arms around him. He held her close, as Nathaniel let them know it was time.

"I know we're not married, but I need you standing up there with me, if you're willing."

"Of course, my angel."

Eden stood to the side of the caskets, Johnny by her side. Eden watched as the doors opened. She felt a bit of comfort when she saw Mikael, Hannah, Dean, and Alex among the first people to enter. They got in line, giving both Johnny and Eden hugs as they passed through. The four of them sat down together. Even though they didn't know Eden's parents, they stayed to support their friend.

Eden tensed up when she saw Todd's parents, but Emily was civil today, likely because they were in public. Whatever the reason, Eden was thankful. Wave after wave of mourners came through. Eden recognized some of them, and while everyone was civil, she swore she could see scornful looks from quite a few of them. It was slowing down as it got closer to the time for the service.

One of the last mourners to come through was a couple close in age to her parents. She said nothing other than that she was sorry. Eden felt a strange connection to her, though she was positive they'd never met.

Nathaniel let her know the last people had come through, so she and Johnny sat down. A few minutes later, the minister from the church her parents attended walked up front. The service was only 30 minutes and there was no mention made of Eden other than a comment about them having an estranged child. She was hurt, but not surprised. Johnny kept his hand on hers the whole time. Once the service was done, everyone paid their last respects, then headed out to wait for the processional to the cemetery.

Dean, Alex, Mikael, and Hannah waited until everyone else had left the room. They walked up front with Eden and Johnny, the six of them standing there, watching as the funeral home staff approached the caskets.

"Miss Mitchell, when you're ready, the limo is waiting. We'll close the caskets and bring them out to the lead car."

Eden approached the caskets, gave her parents one last look and returned to her friends.

"I'm ready," Eden said.

The group walked outside. Eden and Johnny got into the limo while their friends went to their cars. Once the two caskets had been loaded into the lead car, the procession started the ride to the cemetery. When they arrived. Johnny stepped out of the limo and escorted Eden to the gravesite. There were two chairs setup, so Johnny and Eden sat down. Richard and Emily approached, so Johnny stood. He gestured to the chair so Emily could sit. She pulled her chair away from Eden and sat down. Richard shook Johnny's hand. Once the rest of the mourners reached the site, the minister did a short ceremony, then invited everyone to place flowers on the caskets.

Emily was about to cut in front of Eden when Richard grabbed her arm. Eden and Johnny laid their flowers on the caskets, then stepped aside. They remained until the other mourners finished. Richard approached them.

"I'd like to apologize for my wife's behavior," Richard said.

"No need. I understand her anger. I was horrible to her son."

"I appreciate your humility, but I am aware of what happened, and while I said nothing to keep up appearances, I understand why you left. Thank you for handling her digs with such grace."

"I know it's not the same as losing as her son, but I understand that she's feeling grief. Sniping back at her would've accomplished nothing. I wish you both the best."

"Thank you."

Eden nodded as she watched Richard and Johnny shake hands before he and Emily walked to their car. Alex and Hannah both gave Eden a big hug, followed by Dean and Mikael. Once everyone else was gone, Eden sat down for a moment. Johnny sat next to her and took her hands.

"You're doing great, baby. It won't be much longer."

Eden nodded, her eyes filling with tears as she gazed at her man.

"Thank you for being my knight in shining armor. I keep expecting to see you on a white horse," she said, a small smile forming on her lips.

He bowed to her, then took her hand, and they walked back to the limo. There was a large crowd at the restaurant, including the tent area, but Hannah had held two seats for them at a table up front. As they made their way over to the table, Max's mother stopped them. She gave Eden a warm hug.

"I'm so very sorry, sweetie. If there's ever anything I can do, please let me know. I love you like a daughter," she said.

"Thank you so much. I love you and your amazing son so much."

She gave Johnny a hug and told him to take good care of Eden, then went back inside to help her son. They got to the table and sat down in the chairs Hannah had saved. Eden realized she was starving.

"I'll be back. I'm starving, so I need to get something to eat," Eden announced.

"Allow me. I'll be right back with two plates," Mikael said.

"Thank you."

Johnny went with him so he could grab something to drink for himself and Eden.

"How's she doing?" Mikael asked.

"As best as expected. I think tonight is going to be rough. She's been occupied with everything going on today, but when we get home, I'm preparing for her to break down."

"I'm glad she has you to help her through it."

"I'm never going anywhere. In fact, prior to everything happening, I was thinking of proposing to her. I still plan to, but I want to wait a little while to let her process everything she's been through."

"Congratulations, man. If you need any help when the time comes, let us know."

"Thanks."

They walked back to the table. Mikael put two plates down for Johnny and Eden, then sat back down next to Hannah. She was only about two bites in when Emily came storming over to their table. She stood next to Eden, hands on her hips and a sneer on her face.

"Just as I would have expected, you have no decorum. I guess that's why my son chose your sister instead."

"I beg your pardon."

"Here you sit, feeding your face before you could be bothered to say a little something to your guests."

"I was starving."

"I DON'T CARE," she said right in Eden's face.

Richard, not realizing his wife had left their table, raced over.

"Emily, stop this at once."

"Little Miss Trailer Trash needs to learn some manners. Thank heavens she wasn't able to have children. I shudder to think what heathens they would have become."

Before anyone else could respond, Eden stood, her face bright red.

"I put up with your side glances and snide remarks for the entire time I was married to your son. Despite the way everything went down, you still saw fit to put all the blame on my shoulders. I accepted that out of respect, but you've crossed a line. It devastated me when I found out I'd never be able to conceive. Instead of supporting me, all of you blamed me for a condition I was born with. I am not now, nor have I ever been trailer trash. I'm an Ivy League educated woman who owns her own business and has an amazing boyfriend and friends. I hold no ill will toward anyone from my past, so please refrain from any more of your comments."

"Listen here, you bitch-" Emily started before Richard interrupted.

"No, you listen. Eden has done nothing to deserve this. Our son treated her terribly. Instead of supporting her, he cheated on her with her sister. Still, she stayed far longer than most. If you should be angry with anyone, it's Todd. Now, get back to our table and leave Eden alone."

Emily stomped off like a petulant child. Richard apologized again, then hurried off to his table. Eden sat down and wouldn't take her eyes off her feet. Her reaction, especially in public, mortified her and at a time like this. Hannah leaned over and whispered to her.

"That was bad-ass. She needed to hear that."

Eden smiled and replied, "It felt kinda good."

The rest of the luncheon was much less eventful. The crowd dissipated, leaving the six friends and the restaurant staff. Eden tried to help cleanup, but Max was having none of that. He hired extra staff to help, so he had everything covered. She thanked Max for everything, then headed away from the restaurant.

"Where are you going?" Johnny asked.

"Since the limo left, I have a long walk home," Eden said.

"Don't be silly, we'll drive you both home," Hannah said.

"You've already done more than enough," Eden said.

Hannah nodded at Johnny, who walked over, put Eden over his shoulder and carried her to Mikael's truck. Mikael opened the door and Johnny put her in, then slid in next to her. She smiled, grateful that they had such great friends, but she was feeling a little guilty.

"I appreciate this, but I feel like all I've done is take, take, take," Eden said.

"Nonsense. This is what friends do. We love you and we love Johnny, so it's our pleasure to do everything we can. We wish it was better circumstances, but we are happy to help," Hannah said.

Mikael pulled into Johnny's driveway. They got out and hugged Eden and Johnny, then headed home. As Johnny was unlocking the door, Eden let out an enormous yawn. They headed inside and got ready for bed. They were lying together, Johnny holding her in his arms. He felt a dampness on his chest and saw tears spilling over. He just held her tight as she released everything that she had gone through. He took his thumb and wiped her tears.

"I love you, my angel."

"Johnny, I love you more than words could ever say."

She went to the bathroom to wash her face, then got back in bed. She nestled herself back in Johnny's arms and fell asleep. Johnny followed, neither of them moving until the following morning. After breakfast, they were sitting in the living room.

"I've been thinking about what I want to do," Eden announced.

"Regarding?"

"The company and the house."

"You never stop amazing me. With everything else that's been happening, you still had time to think about that. What did you decide?"

"I want to sell the house. I have no good memories there. The company I want to keep but with a new CEO named. I was leaning toward selling that as well, but I fear new owners would clean house, and I won't be responsible for people losing their jobs."

"This is why I trusted you with my heart. You, my love, are the kindest, most amazing, not to mention sexiest woman I've ever known."

"And you are incredible. Your quiet strength melts my heart, and that sexy body melts my panties. Please take me to bed so I can show you how much you excite me."

They re-emerged from the bedroom a couple of hours later, starving from one hell of a sexy workout.

"I could use a night out. Would you maybe like to hit the club tonight?" Eden asked.

"You bet. I'd love to tear up that dance floor with my sexy woman."

"Should we see if the others want to join us?"

"Yeah."

"Great, I'll go call Hannah and Alex."

When she got done with her phone calls, she raced into the living room.

"They all said yes. And guess what! Hannah told me it's disco night at the club. Wanna go hit the thrift shop and find something 70s to wear?"

"I can't believe I'm saying this, but yes, let's go."

"What do you mean?"

"You've opened my world to so much that I've never experienced. Thank you for giving me my life back, angel."

"Trust me, you've done the same for me."

They found the most awesome disco outfits and couldn't wait to show their friends. They all met at the club at 6. Johnny was wearing a suit that made him look like he just finished starring in Stayin' Alive, while Eden was wearing a gold mini-dress covered in sequins along with gold go-go boots. Alex and Hannah looked equally hot, and all eyes were on them when they walked in.

Other than a couple of quick snack and drink breaks, they never left the dance floor. Eden looked so damn hot Johnny could barely control himself. He couldn't wait to get her home.

"Okay, party people, let's take it down the line," the DJ announced, as The Bee Gees hit Stayin' Alive started booming.

Eden and Johnny were the first to go, earning them catcalls and wolf whistles from their friends. They got a couple of turns down the line, and were by far the hottest couple there. They stayed until the club closed. Johnny took a detour on his way home, finding a secluded area to pull his truck into.

"Baby, get your ass in the back seat."

"Mmm, Johnny, are we horny tonight?"

"After watching you in that dress all night? I sure as fuck am, woman."

They climbed into the back seat, and Eden unfastened Johnny's pants. She smiled when she saw he was going commando. Turns out, he wasn't the only one. Eden mounted her knight and slid her pussy down his cock. She bounced up and down on him as he matched her with powerful thrusts until they exploded together. She pressed her lips to his, kissing him with passion. She felt his dick harden inside her, so she fucked him again. They rode each other hard and fast, experiencing several more powerful orgasms until they had nothing left.

"Holy shit, you know how to fuck, woman."

"Mmm, so do you, baby."

"I guess we should head home, but I'm not sure I can move. You wore my ass out, woman!"

"But it felt so damn good, sexy."

They got back in the front seat and head home. They got right in bed and fell asleep, but not before Johnny made her promise she'd wear that outfit for him again. They woke up Sunday morning and were sitting in the kitchen eating breakfast.

"Are you sure about your decisions, baby?"

"I am. I want to take the money we get for the house and use that for our home. As far as the company, I plan on being owner and chairwoman of the board, but I know nothing about the actual business, so I need someone capable of running it. If I know my father, he was grooming someone to takeover, so I'll just need to find out who."

"I'm on board with your decisions. I just wanted to be sure you were certain."

"I am, though I am scared. I've never come close to having as much money as I'm about to and I'm not sure what to do with it. I'm hoping my father's accountant will help me. I would like to put some of it into my restaurant. There's also one either thing I've been thinking about."

"What's that?"

"Reviving your rockstar dream. We no longer need your income, so maybe you could focus on playing."

"I could never take your money."

"Our money. We're in this together and what's mine is yours."

"Baby, let's table that for now. We can talk about that once we get everything sorted out."

"Okay."

After spending a quiet Sunday at home, they spent Monday morning getting ready for their appointment with Mr. Paul. He called that morning to confirm and let her know that her father's accountant would also be present to plan for transferring assets. She had no idea how much her parents had accumulated. A few hours later, Eden and Johnny were sitting in his truck, attempting to process the fact that Eden was now a multi-millionaire.

Chapter Eighteen

They took the rest of the week off to relax after everything they'd been through. Monday morning rolled around fast. Johnny and Eden dragged themselves out of bed, got ready and headed off to work. Johnny helped Eden open up the restaurant before heading across the street. He was going over some inventory sheets when Mikael stopped by.

"Glad to see you back. How's Eden?" Mikael asked.

"She's doing well. She seems to have made peace with everything. Thank you for asking," Johnny said.

"Good news. Speaking of that, have you given any more thought to proposing?"

"I have, and I want to do it soon. I have an appointment at lunchtime to go look at rings."

"That's so awesome."

"Now, I just need to figure out what to do. I want it to be something special."

Mikael was about to respond when Hannah joined them. Johnny went back to work so she could talk to her husband.

"I just heard from Alex that Lizzie and Andy are coming east for a long vacation. Their flight arrives today, and she wants all of us to get together this Saturday night for karaoke at the club," Hannah said.

"Definitely," Mikael said.

"What about you?" she asked Johnny.

"You don't need to ask me because I'm standing here."

"I wasn't. I would love for you and Eden to join us."

"Okay, thanks."

Hannah smiled and headed back to her office.

"Hey, maybe you could propose on stage during karaoke!" Mikael said.

"I like that idea. I may need some help to pull it off, especially keeping it a secret from Eden."

"I have an idea. I can have Hannah include Eden in a girls' night, then the guys can get together and help you plan things out. I can also hide the ring for you. Dean did that for me when I was planning my proposal for your sister."

"Cool, man. Thanks."

"I'll go run it by Hannah and have her run over to ask Eden."

"Okay."

Mikael went to find Hannah. She came bouncing over a few minutes later and gave Johnny a big hug.

"I'm so happy for you two. I'm going over now to talk to Eden about tomorrow night."

"Thanks, sis. One other quick thing. Can you tell her you need me to do an errand at lunchtime?"

"You got it!"

Eden looked up when she heard the door and saw Hannah.

"Hey, Eden, wanted to see if you had plans tomorrow night."

"Nothing specific, why?"

"I'm planning a girls' night and I would love for you to join us. It will be me and Alex, along with our friend Lizzie, who's flying in from LA today."

"That sounds like fun. Thank you for including me."

"I'll let you know the details once I have them."

"Can't wait!"

"Oh, also, Johnny asked me to tell you he won't be over at lunchtime today. My fault, as I need him to run an errand for the shop."

"Thanks for letting me know. I'm sure he needs a break from me anyway after these two weeks."

"I've seen the way he looks at you, so I'm sure that's not true."

"Thanks. There are things I would tell a girlfriend, but I feel odd because he's your brother."

"Probably for the best. If you need to talk to someone about that stuff, I beg you to pick Alex," Hannah said.

"I promise," Eden said.

Hannah texted later that day to let her know they would meet at their favorite pizza place for dinner. She hadn't met Lizzie, but she always followed her music column. As a writer herself, she was looking forward to chatting with her. She grabbed herself some lunch and ate in her office since Johnny wasn't coming in today. What she didn't know was that he was on his way to pick out an engagement ring. He pulled into the parking lot and walked inside.

"Good afternoon, sir. May I help you?" the saleswoman, whose nametag read Diane, asked.

"I made an appointment to purchase an engagement ring."

"Johnny Davidson?"

"Yes."

"Great, let's get started. Follow me please."

"Thank you."

Diane showed Johnny a tray of rings and he zeroed on one that he loved. It was a beautiful one-carat round cut diamond with two smaller diamonds, one on each side. He could see the ring on his angel's hand, so he knew this was the one.

"This one is perfect for her," Johnny said.

"That's beautiful. She's one lucky woman."

"I'm the lucky one."

"Do you have a preference for the box color? We have red, blue, and green."

"I'll take green, please."

"Very well."

Diane put the ring in a felt green box and walked Johnny down to the cash register. She rang the ring up and let Johnny know the total. He paid for the ring and thanked Diane for her help, then headed back to work. When he got back, he showed the ring to Mikael and Hannah. Mikael shook his hand while Hannah squealed and hugged him. Mikael agreed to hold on to the ring until Saturday, so Eden wouldn't see it.

When he finished for the day, Johnny walked across the street to see if Eden was ready to head home. They still had some of the food left that their friends had brought over, so they hung out at home. Eden never complained about that, as it often ended with them getting naked and trying to set their bed on fire. After Eden said goodnight to Max and the rest of the staff, she and Johnny went home. After they ate dinner, they changed into their comfy clothes and went to the living room to relax with some TV.

"Are you planning on spending less time at the restaurant now?" Johnny asked.

"I've been thinking about that. I need to talk to Max before I decide. If he feels like he can handle being in charge overall, I'd like to pull back and focus more on my writing. What about you? Have you given any more thought about turning your focus back to your music career?"

"I'm still not sure. I hate to just abandon Hannah at the store. I need to think through that some more and then I'll want to talk to them before I do anything."

"I'm glad you're at least thinking about it."

"Thanks, baby."

After a couple hours of watching TV, Eden's hands started wandering onto Johnny's sexy chest. She crushed her lips to his, sliding her tongue into his mouth. He felt his dick stirring. He loved feeling her soft hands on his skin and he wanted her so badly.

"Let's go to bed," she purred.

She giggled as Johnny ran to the bedroom. Pajamas flew everywhere, and they got into bed. They held each other tight, making love until they had nothing left. They fell asleep still naked, neither of them waking until the alarm on Johnny's phone let them know it was time to get ready for work. Eden was looking forward to tonight. She loved having girlfriends to spend time with. She couldn't help but wonder what the guys would do without their women.

"So, are you sure you're going to be okay by yourself tonight?"

"Actually, I won't be. Dean invited all the guys over while you ladies are off having fun."

"Oh, that sounds like fun."

"Not as much fun as being in bed with you, baby!"

"Mmmm, so sexy, my Johnny."

They finished getting ready and headed off to work. They got home and showered together, then got ready for their evenings out. Once the limo picked up Eden, Johnny drove over to Dean's house. Mikael was already there when he arrived, as was Andy.

"Johnny, this is Andy York, a longtime friend of mine from LA. Andy, this is Johnny Davidson," Dean said.

"Nice to meet you," Andy said.

"Likewise," Johnny said.

"So, I hear from Dean that you're getting ready to propose," Andy said.

"I am, and I'm a nervous wreck. I love Eden so much."

"Any idea what you're planning to do?"

"I want to do it at the club on Saturday night during karaoke."

"Any idea what song?" Mikael asked.

"Eden loves David Coverdale, so I was thinking of All I Want All I Need."

"Good choice," Dean said.

"I have an idea how you all can help, if you're willing," Johnny said.

"Shoot," Mikael said.

"If we all go up as a group and bring the women up on stage with us, would you each be willing to sing a song to your woman, so Eden won't suspect anything when I sing to her? I would go last and propose when I'm done."

The other guys all agreed to the plan, making Johnny feel a little less nervous. He just hoped that Eden wouldn't say no or be upset that he asked her in public. They all headed into the living to put the baseball game on when the pizza delivery guy arrived with a couple pies and a couple six-packs of beer. After they ate, Andy had an announcement.

"There's a reason other than vacation that Lizzie and I are here."

"What's up?" Dean asked.

"Alex had to retire, as he was having vocal chord issues, so Damon and Chris split off and formed their own band. Things had been tense for a while, so I'm not surprised they didn't ask me to join. Lizzie and I talked at length about what we wanted to do, and we're moving east. So get ready, you're getting a couple of new townies."

"I'm sorry to hear about Alex and the issues with the band, but we're glad to have you here," Dean said.

"Hey, we could form our own band. We have a singer, guitarist, bassist, and drummer right here in this room," Mikael said.

"That's interesting that you said that, as Eden was just talking to me about getting back into music," Johnny said.

"I'd be down for that," Andy said.

"Me too," Dean said.

"We sure would have the four hottest groupies in the world," Mikael said.

They all agreed how lucky they were to have that amazing group of women in their lives. They all started talking about what said women were doing at that moment. They were very cryptic about their plans for their night out. They wanted the men to think they were up to no good, but in reality, they were going to a wine and painting event. None of them was a talented artist, but they were all damn good at drinking wine. Alex booked them on erotica night, so they each came home with their attempt at painting a cock.

The limo dropped them off in front of Dean's house. They were all standing outside, comparing their artwork and laughing so loudly the men could hear them outside. They were so loud, they didn't even hear the door open. A chorus of loud throat clears quieted them down.

"Dare I ask," Dean said.

All four women hid their artwork behind their backs. Each of the guys walked over to his woman, trying to get their hands on what the women were hiding. The women were laughing as they tried to evade the men. They ended up losing the battle, and the men went inside to see what all the laughing was about. The men pretended to be offended, but all ended up admitting how much they loved having such dirty-minded women in their lives.

"So, what did you guys talk about while we were painting dicks?" Eden asked.

"Oh, you know, just dude stuff," Dean said.

"Fine, don't tell us. We wouldn't want to know anyway," Alex said.

After a little more teasing and laughing, the couples all headed home. Johnny kept teasing Eden about her painting, pretending he was jealous of the picture. Eden promised to show him he had nothing to worry about when they got home. When they got inside, they only made it into the living room before Eden had her hands all over Johnny.

"I need to be naked with you right now," Eden said.

"Damn, woman, I want you."

They disappeared into their bedroom and didn't reemerge until morning. The rest of the week dragged on, as Johnny was excited to ask Eden to marry him. He had talked to the other guys and worked out what he needed them to do. Now he just had to hope that Eden said yes. Saturday morning rolled around and Johnny was trying to stay calm, so she didn't get suspicious. He couldn't wait to sing to her, and he was especially excited for his encore!

Dean let the club's owner know what they had planned so he could call the group up on stage at the start of karaoke. Mikael had the ring and Hannah was sneaking a bouquet of sunflowers into the club. Johnny booked a romantic hotel room for them to celebrate in. He waited until Eden was in the shower to pack an overnight bag and hide it in his truck. It was time for them to head to the club, and Johnny could barely catch his breath.

Everyone else was already there when Johnny and Eden arrived. Johnny had arranged that so they could hide anything he needed for the proposal. They walked over to the table and sat down. A waiter came over and took their drink order while they waited for Karaoke to start. Dean already took care of ordering appetizers for the table. Johnny was too nervous to eat, but he had to force something down. He was doing everything he could to keep Eden from suspecting that anything was happening.

When it was time for karaoke to start, Doug walked onto the stage.

"Dudes and dudettes, we have a special treat for you tonight. We have some fan-favorites with us tonight. Please welcome them to the stage."

"That's our cue," Dean announced, so everyone got up and headed up to the stage.

"What's going on?" Alex asked, pretending she didn't know.

"You'll see," Dean winked.

Dean grabbed the microphone and pointed at the chair setup in front of the Karaoke machine. Alex sat down and Dean sang a love song to her. Andy and Mikael followed suit with Lizzie and Hannah. Last up was Johnny. Eden sat down in the chair. She kept her eyes on Johnny the entire time he sang, so she didn't see Hannah grab the sunflowers. When Johnny was done, he walked over and stood in front of Eden.

"Eden, my love, my angel, you've affected my life in ways I didn't think were possible. I came alive when I met you and I can barely remember my life before you. I love you more than I've ever loved anyone."

He made eye contact with Hannah, who walked over and handed the sunflowers to Eden. When Eden turned back to Johnny, he was down on one knee.

"Eden, will you marry me?" Johnny asked as he opened the green velvet box he was holding.

"Oh my god. Yes, Johnny, I'll marry you. I love you."

Johnny put the ring on her finger. He stood up and pulled her up, wrapping her in his arms. He kissed her as the entire club burst into applause. Their friends rushed over and pulled them into a huge group hug. They walked off the stage, but instead of returning to their table, Dean led them to the dressing room area. He opened the door to the room. They had decorated the room with balloons and a large banner that read Congratulations, Johnny and Eden. There was a bottle of champagne and eight glasses. Mikael popped the bottle open and poured everyone a glass.

"A toast to Johnny and Eden. Congratulations on your engagement," Mikael toasted.

"To Johnny and Eden," the rest of the group said in unison.

After everyone drank their champagne, Johnny addressed the group.

"Thank you all so much for helping me plan this amazing night. Most of all, thank you to my love for saying yes. I love you so much, my angel."

"I love you more than anything, my sexy man."

"Ready to get out of here?"

"Where are we going?"

"I rented us a very sexy hotel room."

"Oooh, let's go!"

The other ladies laughed at how eager she was, but they all understood. They all loved spending naughty time with their men. Johnny and Eden thanked their friends for everything, then ran to his truck and raced to the hotel Johnny booked. They got up to their room and went inside. Johnny put the do not disturb sign on the door then turned some music on.

"Dance with me, baby," Johnny said as he pulled Eden into his arms.

He crushed his lips to hers as they swayed to the music. She slid her tongue in his mouth, exploring as she felt a familiar heat building between her thighs. She ran her hands down Johnny's back to that sexy ass of his, squeezing hard. She could feel his erection straining against his pants as he held her tight. She unfastened his pants and slid her hand inside, stroking his hard cock.

"Fuck, I want you, woman," he said.

"I want you too. Please come to bed with me," she purred.

He followed her to the bed, his eyes never leaving that sexy little ass as she swayed her hips. Damn, that woman was beautiful, he thought to himself.

"I need to taste that hot dick."

She crawled over to Johnny and got on all fours. She wrapped her lips around his cock, sliding her mouth up and down his long, thick shaft. She moaned when she felt his fingers stroking her clit, swollen with desire. She teased his balls with her fingers while she sucked him hard.

"Holy fuck, woman, you're so damn good at that."

She moaned as she rocked her hips, the feeling of his fingers massaging her pussy driving her wild.

"Baby, get on your back. It's my turn to taste you."

"Oh, Johnny," she cooed.

Eden rolled onto her back and spread her legs wide. Johnny ran his tongue between her sexy breasts and down her soft stomach. She gasped when she felt his tongue slide into her folds.

"Fuck, you're so wet, baby. You taste so damn sweet."

He swiped his tongue up and down her pussy, stopping to suck her clit. She gasped and moaned as she ran her fingers through his hair, holding his head in place while his tongue pleasured her pussy. It was so intense, her body was writhing and bucking beneath him. He slid his hands under her ass and lifted her off the bed.

"Oh god, Johnny, I need your cock deep inside my pussy. NOW!"

He slid up her body, kissing her hard so she could taste her sweet honey on his tongue. He slid a pillow under her, giving him the angle he needed to penetrate her even deeper. Fuck, it always felt incredible inside that hot woman. He groaned as he slid his dick in and out of her slick tunnel.

"Please let me ride you," she said.

He laid down and wagged his finger at her. She mounted him, sliding down his cock, taking him in deep. She rode him hard, her sexy tits bouncing in his face. The sight of his sexy woman, now his fiancée, on top of him, was so damn hot. He sucked her tits, his tongue flicking her hard nipples as she came undone around him.

"Oh, fuck, so good, Johnny."

Watching her let loose and come for him sent him over the edge and he shot a load of hot cream deep inside her. She laid down next to him and spread her legs. He watched her slide her finger inside her pussy, then slide it into her mouth.

"Mmmm, tastes so good," she said.

"I might need to stop calling you angel. You're becoming quite the sexy little devil."

"Thanks to all your hot lovin', baby."

She slid next to him and laid her head on his chest. He pulled her in close and kissed her.

"I'm so happy you said yes. I was a nervous wreck all day."

"You hid it well. It caught me completely off-guard since the other guys also sang to their women."

"Exactly what we planned."

"So, is that what you guys discussed while I was out with the girls?"

"Among other things."

"Anything you can share? I don't want you to go against bro code," she said.

"Ask me again tomorrow."

"Why tomorrow?"

"Because right now, I wanna fuck again."

"Oh, Johnny."

They spent the rest of the night in bed, celebrating their engagement.

Chapter Nineteen

Johnny and Eden slept in after one hell of a night, enjoyed some room service for breakfast, then headed home. Eden was still on cloud nine after the proposal, but she hadn't forgotten that Johnny promised to tell her something.

"So, now that we're on our way home, you still need to tell me what else you guys talked about the other night," Eden said to Johnny.

"Mikael joked that the four of us could start a band, but it got me to thinking. Why couldn't we? And even if the four of us didn't do it together, I wanna play."

"You don't know how happy that makes me."

"I don't think I could be happier than I am right now - at least until we get married."

She looked over at him, the biggest smile on her beautiful face.

"I never thought I would be happy again until I met you."

"So, my turn now to ask you something."

"Of course."

"What are you going to do tomorrow? Talk to Max?"

"Yes, I think that needs to be the first thing I do. If he can handle things at least temporarily, then I want to focus on finding the right people to handle things at my father's company."

"You mean your company."

"Right, still getting used to that."

"The other thing I want to get serious about is finding a home."

"I know. It just never seems like there's enough time. Maybe we could start by looking online."

"Let's do that when we get back."

"Okay!"

Once they got home and unpacked, Johnny booted up his laptop. He and Eden sat together looking at local real estate. The first few pages of listings didn't pique their interest. Johnny clicked over to page five and there it was. They looked at each other, both of them smiling widely. He pulled out his cell and dialed the contact number for the agent overseeing the sale. As luck would have it, she was available for a walk-through today.

"Thank you so much, Ms. Johnson. We'll see you in an hour," Johnny said, then disconnected.

"I can't believe it's still available," Eden said.

"There haven't even been any offers yet. I just hope we don't get there and find a lot of issues."

"Me too. The pictures make it look beautiful, but it would be easy enough to pretty those up."

Johnny looked up the address to see how long of a drive it would be. When it came time, they followed their GPS and pulled up to the house, just as the agent, Melissa Johnson, arrived. She greeted them and escorted them inside. The first thing Eden noticed, and fell in love with, was the double doors that led into the house. Her eyes went wide when they walked inside. The foyer was beautiful. There was an entryway to the kitchen on the right, stairs to the second floor rooms on the left, and the living room straight ahead.

The kitchen was enormous, with more cabinet space than Eden had ever seen. There was a pantry and a door that led to the connected four-car heated garage, which also included a half-bath and laundry room. There was also a small cafe table for two. The kitchen was a pale yellow, and the curtains had sunflowers on them. Eden took that as a sign.

The living room was stunning. There was a fireplace, a large wall-mounted TV and large open floor plan. Sliding glass doors led to the backyard, complete with a large deck, and an in-ground swimming pool and hot tub. Eden loved everything she saw so far, and couldn't wait to see the second floor. There was one other door in the living room, but Melissa took them upstairs first.

The second floor featured a master bedroom, a full bath with soaking tub for two and a walk-in glass-enclosed shower stall. There was also a walk-in closet and two other rooms they could use for a variety of purposes. The rooms were each a different rich color, and they were all stunning. When they finished touring the second floor, Johnny and Eden followed Melissa back downstairs.

"I've been saving the best for last," Melissa bubbled.

She opened the door and Eden's jaw dropped. She couldn't believe she was standing there, starting at an indoor swimming pool and hot tub. Off to the side was a bar area, complete with a TV, stereo system, and seating area. Eden and Johnny looked at each other, both of them awestruck at what they just saw. Eden was having a hard time controlling her thoughts, and she started picturing all the different places there were to have some dirty sex in this amazing house.

"So, what do you think?" Melissa asked.

"It's beautiful," Eden said.

"I agree with my angel," Johnny said.

"I'm so pleased. The owners haven't had a bite yet, likely because of the size and the price."

"May we have a few moments to talk?" Eden asked.

"Of course. I'll wait on the front porch."

Once Melissa was outside, Eden asked, "So, do you want to make an offer, or do you want to think about it first?"

"Baby, I saw your face when we were walking around. I know your naughty look. How many rooms did you picture us fucking in?"

"Um, all of them," Eden admitted.

"Me too. I think we should make an offer."

"Let me just make a quick call to my father's lawyer and see if he has any information about this house before we commit ourselves."

Eden told Mr. Paul the address and after a few minutes, he let her know there were no known issues. He agreed with the price and encouraged her to make an offer. She thanked him and let Johnny know what he said.

"I think we can stop leaving Melissa hanging," Eden said.

Johnny opened the door and asked Melissa to come back in.

"We'd like to make an offer," Johnny said.

"List price is 750 thousand. What would you like to offer?"

"We'd like to offer 775 thousand," Johnny said.

"I'll need to see a mortgage approval for that amount before submitting the offer."

"What if we plan to pay cash?" Eden asked.

"Then I'll need proof you have that amount on hand."

Eden showed Melissa the paperwork from her inheritance, which was more than enough to cover the price of the home.

"I'll pass your offer on to the owner and I'll be in touch when I hear."

"Thank you so much," Eden said.

Melissa walked them out and locked up. They shook hands and Melissa repeated she would be in touch once she spoke with the owner. Johnny and Eden sat in his truck for a couple of minutes.

"I love that house. I hope our offer is acceptable," Eden said.

"Me too, baby. How about we head home and you act out some of those dirty thoughts you were having?"

"Mmm, yes please, Mr. Sexy."

They emerged from the bedroom a couple of hours later and went out for pizza. They ordered a large pie and a pitcher of beer, and held hands, gazing at each other while they waited. After they finished eating, they drove over to the park to take a walk. They loved heading back to the lake and sitting on the dock. Johnny looked at his woman, who was sitting there with a dreamy look on her face.

"Okay, spill it. What are you thinking about?"

"Oh, you know, that night we had some dirty, dirty fun back here."

"I thought sol, my sexy devil."

He pulled her close and kissed her hard. She felt herself getting wet. If it hadn't still been light out, she may have ripped his clothes off and fucked him hard right there on the dock. They were so lost in their kiss, they didn't hear footsteps approaching until a couple of throat clears broke their kiss. They looked up and saw Andy and Lizzie standing there.

"I get it. I was that way with this guy," Lizzie said, pointing to Andy.

"Impossible to resist those sexy rockers," Eden said.

"Mind if we sit for a few minutes?" Lizzie asked.

"Not at all," Eden said.

Andy and Johnny started talking about music, so Lizzie turned to Eden.

"I didn't get much of a chance to chat with you the other night, but I love that you're also a writer. Have you thought about publishing anything?" Lizzie asked.

"I've thought about it, but I wasn't sure I was good enough."

"I get that. I felt that way when I first started out. Landing this job helped build my confidence."

"That's so great. I love reading your column every week. I'm all about the smut."

"I'd love to read some of your work sometime."

"Wow, really? I'd love that."

"My pleasure. So, I have to ask you, you seemed to be enjoying the dock. Any special reason."

"Umm, we may have done some dirty stuff here one night."

"I knew I liked you. Andy and I did it on a beach."

"Ooh, fun. I haven't done that yet. Might have to drop some hints to Johnny."

They started giggling, prompting Andy and Johnny to question what they found so funny.

"Girl talk," Lizzie and Eden said in unison.

"We probably wouldn't want to know anyway," Andy said.

"Let's let the lovebirds get back to their kissing," Lizzie said.

After Andy and Lizzie left, Johnny and Eden did just that. Johnny crushed his lips to hers and slid his tongue into her mouth. She moaned as their tongues danced, her desire building until she felt a wetness between her legs.

"We need to go home right now," Eden said.

"Why so eager, my angel?"

"I need you inside me."

"Oh, baby, let's go."

They raced out of the park and sped home, their desire for each other reaching its boiling point as they raced into the house and into the bedroom. Clothes flew everywhere in a frenzy. Eden pointed to the bed, so Johnny laid down. She climbed on top of him and took him inside. Her pussy was so wet with desire that he slid into her with ease.

"Fuck, you feel so good, baby," Johnny said.

"I love the way your dick feels inside me," Eden purred.

She leaned back, using his muscular thighs for support as she fucked him. He took a couple of fingers and started rubbing her clit, making her moan even louder.

"That's it, baby, bounce for me. Fuck, you look so damn good ridin' me."

"Oh, Johnny, so fuckin' good. Oh god, oh fuck, holy shit," she screamed as her love rained down on him, soaking his cock with her powerful orgasm.

"Holy shit, woman, that was so fucking hot," he said as he emptied himself inside her.

They were laying together basking in the afterglow of their passion. Eden loved laying in Johnny's strong, sexy arms.

"So, tomorrow's the big day. Do you want me there when you talk to Max?"

"I should be fine alone, but if you would like to stay, you're more than welcome."

"Okay, baby."

"Thank you," Eden said, then let out a loud yawn.

"Tired, baby?"

"Mmm, all that bouncing."

"And you looked damn good doing it, woman."

"I love you. You really are my hero."

"I love you, my beautiful angel."

They fell asleep, still holding each other, and didn't stir until the alarm went off the following morning.

Chapter Twenty

Eden was nervous to talk to Max. She was unsure how he was going to react, and she hoped he would see it as an opportunity for him to advance and not Eden abandoning him. Max was already at the restaurant when Eden and Johnny arrived.

"Good Morning, lovebirds," Max said.

"Good Morning," Eden said. "Before you get started, could you come sit? Johnny and I need to fill you in on some stuff."

"Sure."

"While I was out, I met with my father's attorney, and because of my sister also passing, I'm the sole heir to their assets, including my dad's company. I'm going to need to spend some time there finding the right people to run things, which means more time away from here."

"Wow. That must have been a bit of a shock."

"To say the least."

"What does this mean for me? Are you closing the restaurant?"

"I don't want to, which is why I wanted to talk to you. How would you like to be in charge of everything? You would have the freedom to make hiring decisions, and anything else I was doing. I will still take care of payroll and I would just want you to keep me informed."

"You would trust me with that?"

"Without a doubt. You've more than proved you're capable. And of course, I will increase your salary."

"I accept. It's always been my dream to run a restaurant, so this is amazing. Thank you for your faith in me. And oh my god, I just saw your finger. When did that happen?"

"I asked her this past Saturday night," Johnny said.

"Congratulations!"

"Thank you," Eden said. "For now, though, we better get things ready before our diners arrive."

"Will you be here all day today?" Max asked.

"I'll be leaving mid-morning, as I need to head over to my new company. I will split time between the two places until I go over everything with you and make sure you're comfortable."

"Sounds like a plan," Max said, then headed off to the kitchen.

"I need to head across the street," Johnny said.

"Okay. Are you going to talk to Hannah and Mikael today?"

"Yes. Not sure what I'm going to do yet about the job, but I want to fill them in."

"Good luck. I wish I could be with you, but I need to stay here then head over to my meeting."

"I understand. I hope everything goes well at your meeting."

"Thanks."

Johnny gave his woman a hug and kiss goodbye, then headed over to work. He was a little nervous about talking to Hannah and Mikael. He wasn't planning to quit, but he had been thinking more and more about trying to pursue music again. For now, he planned just to tell them about Eden's new fortune and see how they react. He was so grateful to his angel for reawakening his love of music, not to mention all the other things she helped him with. Johnny got in right after Hannah and Mikael and asked if he could speak with them.

"What's up? You seem serious," Hannah asked.

"Well, Eden got quite a shock when we met with her father's lawyer. Because her sister also passed in the accident, she became the sole heir to her parents' assets. That means their house, her father's company, everything. Eden's now a multi-millionaire."

"Wow. What is she going to do?" Hannah asked.

"She talked to Max today about him running the restaurant. She will maintain ownership, but she wants him to manage it. She is also planning to stay on as owner of her dad's company, but she doesn't want to be CEO or anything like that, so she's going to be doing some hiring."

"What about you?" Mikael asked.

"I don't know. Even before you joked about it the other night, she had been encouraging me to get back into music, but I don't want to just up and leave the store after you gave me this opportunity."

"Interesting that you mention that," Hannah said. "Mikael is also thinking about getting back into playing."

"Maybe we need to have a serious talk with Dean and Andy," Mikael said.

"How about tonight?" Johnny said.

Mikael grabbed his phone and dialed Dean's number.

"Yo," Dean said.

"Can you call Andy and the two of you meet at my place tonight, around 7?" Mikael asked.

"Yeah. Everything okay?"

"Yeah."

"Cool."

They disconnected, and Hannah rolled her eyes.

"What, babe?" Mikael asked.

"That conversation would have gone way different if it had been women," she said.

"For now, I'm going to hold off on deciding about what I do here," Johnny said.

"Sounds like a plan," Mikael said.

Johnny headed over to the record shop to get things ready for the day. Meanwhile, Eden was waiting for the breakfast rush to ease so she could head over to her dad's company. Her father's attorney would meet her there. The plan was first to meet with her father's second in command, then address the rest of the senior staff. Once all they made the decisions, she would address the full staff. She had to admit she was nervous, but felt better that Mr. Paul would be with her. When Eden arrived, Mr. Paul was waiting for her in the lobby. She hadn't been to her father's company since she was a child, and a lot had changed since then.

"Good Morning, Eden," Mr. Paul said.

"Good Morning, Mr. Paul."

"Larry is fine."

"Okay."

"I think we should first head to your father's office so you can get acclimated."

They walked down to her father's office. Eden couldn't believe how big it was. She gasped when she saw the table that housed some personal pictures. She saw a framed newspaper clipping announcing the debut of Garden of Eden.

"Your father was proud of what you accomplished," Larry said.

"Then why did he never tell me?"

"Pride. He was too stubborn to admit he was wrong about you."

"Thank you for telling me."

"Of course. That's why I wanted to bring you here alone first."

"I appreciate that. So, who are we meeting with first?"

"Your father's second in command, Olivia Benson. She's Penn educated. She's strong, driven, and more than capable of running this company."

"She sounds like the leading candidate to become CEO."

"I believe she is. I wanted to discuss how your father interviewed and see how you wish to proceed."

"Okay."

"He preferred that I ask the questions so that he could observe the candidate. Of course, I'm open to your preference, but we always had excellent results using that method."

"I would like to proceed the way my father did, especially since my knowledge is limited. I am, however, good at reading people, so having my focus there will help."

A knock on the office door interrupted them. Larry walked over and opened the door.

"Miss Mitchell, I'm Rose, your father's, I apologize, I mean your, executive assistant."

"No apologies necessary. I remember seeing you at the service. It will take some time to break that habit. I still think of this as my father's company. And please, call me Eden."

"Thank you for being so understanding, Eden. I have the coffee cart for your upcoming meeting."

Eden walked over to get the cart, having that same feeling of connection she felt when Rose paid her respects at the funeral.

"I'm happy to set it up."

"Okay," Eden said. "I own a restaurant, so it's my instinct to do that. Please bear with me."

Rose smiled, then set up the coffee cart, which was complete with hot and cold water and several varieties of pastry.

"Shall I let Ms. Benson know you're ready for her, or do you need more time?"

Eden looked at Larry. He nodded and said, "You can let her know. Thank you."

Rose walked out and a few moments later, returned with Olivia in tow. She introduced Eden and asked if anyone wanted coffee or something to eat. Everyone wanted coffee, so Rose poured and served three cups, then excused herself. Larry positioned himself between Eden and Olivia and began the interview.

Eden watched and listened as Larry and Olivia conversed, making small notes for herself. Olivia impressed her. Olivia knew the company well, and she seemed more than capable of moving into the CEO position. Once Larry finished his questions, he gave Olivia the chance to ask any she may have.

"Not at this time. I would just like to say to you, Eden, that I'm sorry for your loss," Olivia said.

"Thank you, I appreciate that," Eden said.

"We'll be in touch, Ms. Benson," Larry said.

"Thank you," Olivia said, then turned and left the office.

"So, what do you think, Eden?" Larry asked.

"I think she's perfect for the job. I'd like to offer her the position before I leave today, unless there's paperwork that needs to be done first."

"Let me see if the necessary parties are available."

"Okay."

Larry made some phone calls while Eden enjoyed another cup of coffee and her weakness, a small cheese Danish. She sat and looked around again at her father's personal items. She still couldn't believe he had a framed copy of the article about her restaurant. Larry's voice interrupted her thoughts.

"I spoke with the VP of Human Resources. We can offer her the position today. He's sending a member of his staff up to help us prepare the offer letter. Once we do that, we can call Ms. Benson back in and offer her the job."

"That's great. It will be an enormous weight off my shoulders to know we can keep my father's company going."

"Can I offer you a small bit of advice?"

"Of course."

"Get in the habit of calling it your company. I know it's a lot to take in, but you do, in fact, own this business now."

"I know. I'm working on it," she said.

"Excuse me, Miss Mitchell, Mr. Paul. Toby from HR is here," Rose announced.

"Please send him in," Eden said.

Eden sat down at her desk, Larry and Toby sitting across from her. She typed up the offer letter as Toby instructed her what to include. He checked it over when she was done and confirmed everything was in order. Larry asked Rose to have Olivia to return to the office. They all sat at the round conference table in the office. Toby presented a copy of the offer to Olivia while Larry reviewed it with her. Eden smiled when Olivia's face lit up after they offered her the position.

"I'm honored that you've selected me," Olivia said.

"You impressed me," Eden said. "I'm confident you'll do a wonderful job."

"Thank you."

"Since we're into the afternoon, why don't we reconvene in the morning and start talking strategy? I also would like to announce it to the senior staff tomorrow," Larry said.

"I agree," Olivia said.

"Then it's a plan," Eden said.

After Olivia and Toby left the office, Larry asked Eden if she needed anything else.

"I'm just going to stay for a little while and look around. Then I'll be heading home, so you're more than welcome to do the same."

"Enjoy the rest of your day."

"Thank you for all your help."

Eden was sitting at her father's desk when her cell rang. She smiled when she saw Johnny's handsome face.

"Hey, sexy," she said.

"Hey, beautiful. How'd it go today?"

"I have a lot to tell you tonight."

"Same here."

"I'm getting ready to leave the office now. See you soon."

"Can't wait."

After Eden disconnected, she locked up the office and headed home. All she could think about was being in Johnny's arms. She was just pulling into the garage when he pulled in. They got inside and he pulled her close, kissing her hard. They walked into the bedroom so Eden could change into jeans and a t-shirt. Johnny watched as his angel removed her clothes. He loved her silky skin, and he planned to show her how much later.

After they changed, they cooked dinner and sat down at the table.

"How was your day, dear?" Johnny said.

"Eventful. But good news, I found the new CEO. My dad's second in command, Olivia, was perfect for the job. The plan for tomorrow is to talk strategy, then announce her promotion to senior leadership. I'm hoping after that and announcing to the full staff, I'll be able to step back."

"That's awesome, babe."

"Now, tell me about your day, Mr. Sexy."

"Well, it was interesting. I'm meeting Mikael, Dean, and Andy at Mikael's house at 7. We're going to talk to Dean and Andy about forming a band."

"Oh my god, I'm so happy to hear that," Eden squealed.

"I owe it all to you, baby."

"I love you."

"I love you too. When we get home from Mikael's, I intend to show you how much!"

"Mmm."

Johnny and Eden headed over to Mikael's a little before 7 and were the first to arrive. A couple of minutes later, the rest of the group arrived.

"I'm sure you're wondering why we asked you to come over," Mikael said to Dean and Andy.

They both nodded yes, so Mikael continued.

"Johnny and I were talking this morning and we are interested in putting a band together. Of course, you are the two we want to round out our foursome."

Eden watched as Alex's and Lizzie's faces lit up with excitement.

"What do you guys think?" Johnny asked.

"I love the thought of being able to sing again," Dean said.

"I've been so down since Dark Horse split up. You don't know how much this has picked me up. Count me in!" Andy said.

"We need to celebrate. How about Saturday night at the club?" Eden announced.

"Maybe we could announce the band and perform?" Johnny said.

"Then I think we need to come up with a name," Mikael said.

"We want input from everyone, including you sexy women," Dean said. "But for now, let's see what the Flyers are doing."

Mikael turned the TV on. They all turned their attention to the game, but their minds were all spinning after the decision to form a band. The game went to a commercial and, without warning, Eden squealed.

"Look, look, look at this commercial for Stardust Casinos," Eden said.

"You like that place or something, babe?" Johnny asked.

"Never been there, but Stardust, oh my god. I love that as a name for the band."

The look on everyone's face showed Eden that they all loved it.

"Ladies and gentleman, I give you Stardust," Hannah announced.

Everyone was cheering and laughing, all of them elated at this new chapter in their lives. Johnny pulled his angel into his arms and whispered in her ear.

"Thank you for having us over, Mikael, but we need to go," Eden said.

"What did you say to her, man?" Dean said.

Johnny flashed a wicked smile, but didn't say a word. He and Eden said quick goodbyes as she ran for the door, to the amusement of their friends. Johnny sped home and the second they got inside, clothes started flying. Johnny picked his angel up and put her over his shoulder. He carried her off to the bedroom. He laid her down on the bed, joined her, and before she could say a word, his lips were on hers. He jammed his tongue in her mouth as she moaned and writhed beneath him.

"Fuck, I want you, woman."

"Oh, Johnny, I want to feel you moving inside me."

"In due time, my love, but first, I want to pleasure you."

"Mmm, yes, please."

Johnny was craving the taste of his sweet woman, so instead of teasing her like he usually did, he slid his tongue into her folds. He ran his tongue up and down her pussy, stopping to suck on her clit. She bucked her hips beneath him as he licked her harder.

"Oh god, so good, oh, Johnny," she called out.

He sucked her clit hard until her entire body quivered beneath him. There was little he loved more than making his woman explode with his touch. All he could think about now was having his dick inside his beautiful angel. He slid up her body, glistening after her intense orgasm, and slid inside her. He felt her arms wrap around him as he thrusted in and out of her.

"Baby, nothing feels as incredible as being inside you. I love you."

"Oh, Johnny, I love you."

His slow thrusts were replaced by faster ones as he emptied himself deep inside her, growling as he filled her sweet pussy. He leaned down and kissed her, then laid down next to her and pulled her in tight.

"Mmm, Johnny, so good. What was that for?"

"What do you mean?"

"What you whispered in my ear, silly. That you wanted to thank me with lovemaking."

"Baby, look what you've done since you came into my life. I'm able to love again, and now I'm going to be playing music again. None of that would have been possible without you, my angel. I needed to show my gratitude for your love in my favorite way."

"I can't tell you how much it means to me to hear you say that. You've helped me just as much. You've reminded me how amazing the love of a man can be. More importantly, you helped me with my confidence. Todd eft me feeling so worthless after he cheated on me and my family ostracized me. Then this amazing man showed me how to live again."

They spent the rest of the night naked in each other's arms, thanking each other over and over until they were both devoid of energy.

Chapter Twenty-One

They awoke the following morning, still naked, and still holding each other, both of them feeling an incredible sense of calm after their night of passion.

"Are you going to the restaurant this morning, or just to the firm?"

"Just the firm. Max wanted a chance to open on his own. Do you want some breakfast before you head to work?"

"I'll take more of what I had last night."

"I'm not on the menu, silly."

"You're on mine always, baby."

"I would love to show you the office. Would you maybe want to see it sometime?"

"I'd love to."

"I'm going to spend the entire day there today, so maybe you could meet me there when you're done with work."

"Then grab dinner after?"

"Sounds good. After that, we can come home and have dessert."

"And what's for dessert?"

His mouth watered as she looked him up and down and licked her lips. She walked over and kissed him hard, his dick stirring at her sexy touch.

"You, of course, my sexy drummer!"

"How about an appetizer right now?"

"You'll be late for work."

"And?"

"You'll just have to wait until later."

"You're killing me, woman!"

She flashed him a flirty smile as she got out of bed and headed for the shower. Johnny followed and joined her. He grabbed her shower gel and squirted some into her puff. He pulled her in close as he covered her body with floral scented suds. He inhaled deeply, loving her heavenly scent. He finished with strawberry shampoo and conditioner, then rinsed her clean. She sighed, then repeated the same for him. They stood in the hot steamy shower kissing for a long time, attempting to avoid the real world as long as possible.

As they got into separate cars to head to work, Eden couldn't help but imagine a time they'd no longer have to. She spent her ride to work imagining him playing music full time, her by his side supporting him. As long as her businesses were in capable hands, there was no reason that couldn't be reality. She pictured her sexy man on stage shirtless and sweaty, banging away on his drums, and felt a dampening at her core. She couldn't wait to get home later!

Eden spent the rest of the drive attempting to regain her composure and turned her focus to what she hoped to accomplish today. There would be a quick meeting with the senior leads, then a company-wide meeting to announce Olivia as the CEO. Once that was done, Eden planned on visiting each area and spending some time with the leads. Though she would be an owner in name only, she still wanted to at least learn the basics of what they did and get to know the staff that would report to Olivia. She also wanted to spend some time going through her dad's office to see if there was anything she needed to turn over to Olivia.

Eden rode the private executive elevator to the top floor and headed to her office. Rose was just coming out, having setup a coffee cart for her morning meeting with the senior leads.

"Good Morning, Rose. Thank you for the coffee cart."

"Good Morning. My pleasure. Shall I show the attendees in as they arrive?"

"Yes, please."

"Very well."

Rose returned to her desk and waited for the team to arrive. Eden started opening drawers in her desk to see if there was anything she thought Olivia might need. At the bottom of the top right drawer sat a letter with her name on it. She was about to open it when she heard Larry approaching. She couldn't help but wonder what it said, but that would have to wait until later. The rest of the team followed. Larry introduced Eden to the team.

"Thank you, Larry, and thank you to all of you for taking time out of your busy schedules. Please help yourself to coffee and breakfast. I'm sure there's been some uncertainty since my father passed away, but let me assure you, you have nothing to fear. Without further ado, I'd like to introduce you to your new CEO, Olivia Benson."

A round of applause and smiles filled the room, and Eden breathed a sigh of relief as Olivia addressed the staff. She spent about half an hour going through her planned strategy. Eden liked the way she made a point of addressing each lead by name and spending a few minutes discussing their specific function. When she was done, she turned the floor back to Eden.

"As Olivia mentioned, I have taken over as owner and chairwoman of the board. My primary goal was to keep the company in the family, so that everyone still had a job. I would like to spend some time with each of you to learn your area's work, but I will hand over the day-to-day leadership duties to Olivia's more than capable hands. We'll discuss this again with the full staff when we meet with them later this morning. Does anyone have questions?"

As nobody had questions, Eden thanked the group and adjourned the meeting. Olivia and Larry stayed behind to discuss how they would handle meeting with the staff later. Once they had the agenda and the plan determined, Olivia and Larry headed back to their offices until it was time to meet with the full staff. Eden sat down at her desk, feeling a bit overwhelmed.

"Are you okay?" she heard Rose ask.

"Oh, yes, sorry. Just a little lost in thought."

"May I get you some lunch?"

"I appreciate the offer, but I'm fine."

"May I speak honestly for a moment?"

"Of course."

"You're very kind and not at all demanding, very much like your father. It's the reason I've always stayed in this job. Your father spoke highly of you. I believe he wanted to come see you, but your mother wouldn't allow it. He once told me you were the daughter he admired most, as you did not have things handed to you. Your father built this company from the ground up, and he admired hard work."

As her eyes filled with tears, Eden said, "Thank you so much for telling me that."

"You're welcome. Now, why don't you get your face cleaned up while I grab you some lunch?"

"How about instead we go grab lunch together?"

"I would be honored."

After cleaning her face, Eden and Rose headed down to the employee cafeteria. Eden couldn't believe the choice of food the cafeteria offered. She found herself impressed with what her father built, and she was determined to keep it going.

"There's so much to pick from, I don't know what to get," Eden said.

"I enjoy the salad bar. Everything is always fresh and the choices are endless," Rose said.

"Sounds good. I'm going to join you."

After they made their salads, they found an empty table.

"Are you nervous about the staff meeting?" Rose asked.

"I'll admit, a little, but Olivia will do most of the talking, so I think it will be fine."

"I'm sure you will be just fine. I see a lot of your father in you. I hope you don't mind me mentioning him."

"Not at all. I appreciate it."

"So, tell me a little about you."

"Well, prior to all of this, I was just a woman who owned her own restaurant. I plan on keeping it, but I have placed my head chef in charge so I can focus here until I'm sure everything is stable."

"I couldn't help but notice your beautiful ring."

Eden's heart swelled when she looked down at her finger.

"His name is Johnny. He's had quite the upheaval in his life as well. It's what drew the two of us together. We started as friends and eventually fell in love."

"I love a good romance."

"Do you like to read them? I'm writing a book now. I've written a lot of short stories, but this is my first full-length novel."

"Are they steamy?" Rose whispered.

"Very," Eden said, blushing.

"My favorite kind. It's how I've stayed married to the same man for so long."

"What else do you do for fun?"

"I have a book club with my three dearest friends, Dorothy, Blanche, and Sophia. We only read and discuss steamy romance novels like what you write."

"I knew I liked you," Eden said.

They finished their lunch and headed back upstairs. After they got back, Olivia and Larry arrived so they could all enter the meeting room together. After a quick introduction from Larry, Eden filled the staff in on Olivia's promotion to CEO, then turned the microphone over to her. Olivia spent some time running through her talking points and took some questions before adjourning the meeting. They also dismissed the staff early for the day with pay to say thank you.

Eden went back to her office after the meeting. She was feeling a bit tired, but perked up when she heard his voice.

"Good afternoon, sir. May I help you?" she heard Rose say.

"Yes, ma'am. I'm here to see Eden Mitchell."

"You must be Johnny," she smiled.

"I am."

"Eden told me about you. Her face lights up when she speaks about you. She's right through that door, if you'd like to go on in."

"Thank you."

"Eden, will there be anything else today?"

"No, thank you. Please take the rest of the day off and have fun with your husband," she winked.

"Thank you."

Rose smiled as she watched Johnny walk over and give Eden a hug. She closed the office door, giving them some privacy, then headed out.

"How'd today go, baby?" Johnny asked.

"Everything went well."

"You seem a little preoccupied. Is everything okay?"

Eden walked over to her desk and took out the envelope she found earlier.

"I found this in one of the desk drawers this morning."

"Did you read it?"

"I was about to when my dad's lawyer came up for the meeting."

"Do you want to read it now? I can give you some privacy."

"No need for privacy. I would rather you were with me."

"Are you sure?"

"I'm nervous about what it might say."

They sat down on the couch together. Johnny sat in silence while Eden read. She teared up as she read. She folded the letter up and put it back in the envelope.

"I wish he'd told me in person, but at least he wrote it down."

"Something positive, I take it?"

"Yes, he was proud of me. I'll fill you in on details later. Now, though, I believe I promised you something this morning. But first, you need to feed me!"

"Let's go, baby," he said, running for the door.

Eden locked the door behind them. They met at their favorite pizza place for a quick dinner, then headed home for dessert. She didn't wait for Johnny to make a move, grabbing him and crushing her lips to his. He could feel her desire, the way her tongue was exploring his mouth. She unbuttoned his shirt, showering his sexy chest with soft kisses as she exposed his skin.

"Damn, you're sexy," she purred.

All Johnny could muster was a growl as Eden's hands moved down to his belt. She had him out of his pants. She slid her fingers inside the waistband of his underwear and slid them down. She smiled as his erection sprang to life. She backed away from him, eyeing him up and down, licking her lips. After kicking off her shoes, she unbuttoned her blouse and removed it. She ran her hands over her breasts as she removed her bra and swore she saw Johnny drooling.

She reached under her skirt and removed her black lace thong, which she flung at her sexy hunk. After unzipping her skirt, she let it fall to the floor, leaving her standing there naked except for thigh high black stockings. She was about to remove them when Johnny stopped her.

"Please, baby, leave those on. So fucking sexy."

He scooped his goddess up in his arms and carried her into their bedroom.

"I'm in charge tonight," she said when Johnny put her down.

"Fuck, yeah, woman."

"Get that sexy ass in bed. Now!"

Johnny laid down on the bed, his heart racing, anticipating what his angel had in store for him. She straddled his legs and, as she gazed into his eyes, slid her hand between her legs and started pleasuring herself as he watched. He felt like his heart was going to beat out of his chest. He ached to have his cock where her fingers were. As if she could read his mind, she crawled up his body. She grabbed his cock in her hand and lowered her body down on him, taking every inch of his length deep inside her.

"Fuck, it feels like heaven inside you, angel."

"Mmmm, so good, Johnny," she purred.

She slowly rocked her hips, sliding up and down his cock, driving him wild. Nothing felt as incredible as being wrapped around her sexy man, feeling his hands on his back as their bodies became one. Johnny pulled her down so her chest was against his. She crushed her lips to his as they moved together, lost in the magic of their lovemaking until they exploded together. Eden let out a loud sigh as her body went limp against his.

"Oh, Johnny, that felt incredible."

"I love you, my angel."

"I love you too."

Chapter Twenty-Two

Monday morning, Eden drove to the restaurant to check on things. Max was just arriving when she pulled up, so she followed him inside.

"How are things going?" Eden asked.

"Everything has been great. I hired a new cook, so I could focus on managing. Everyone is raving about the food."

"And how have you been? Are you fine without me here?"

"I am. I love this place as if it's my own."

"I'm glad to hear that, as I'm hoping to continue to leave it in your capable hands, if you'd like."

"I would love to. I can't thank you enough for this opportunity."

"You earned it. I'm planning on doing the same at the firm. I want to focus on my wedding and pursuing my writing dream, along with supporting Johnny getting back into music. I will check in and will always be available if something comes up."

"That's awesome. You both already have a number one fan in me."

"You're the best."

Eden grabbed herself coffee and a Danish, hugged Max goodbye and headed off to the firm. She planned to have a similar talk with the leadership team there. She was still thinking about the letter from her father she found. She wished he'd been able to put his pride aside and tell her how he felt, but she was at least grateful that he wrote it. All these years of thinking she was a disappointment, then finding out her father was proud of her helped ease some of the pain she endured growing up. According to what he wrote, it was her mother that was adamant he never tell her.

Something was nagging at her. The letter ended with him saying he needed to tell her the truth about something, but it didn't say what. She felt like she needed to find out and planned to ask Larry later. When Eden got upstairs, she saw Rose already at her desk. She admired her dedication and had a special meeting planned with her in the afternoon.

"Good Morning," Rose said with a warm smile.

"Good Morning," Eden said.

"I've ordered the coffee cart for your meeting with the staff."

"Thank you so much."

"Is there anything you need at the moment?"

"No, thank you. I'm going to get any final preparations ready for the meeting."

"Very well. I'll set up the cart when it arrives."

"Wonderful."

Eden walked into the office, fired up her computer and gazed out the window. The more she thought about writing, the more excited she became. She also loved the idea of getting to go on tour with Stardust. Her mind went back to her fantasy of watching Johnny shirtless and sweaty on stage. She started picturing helping him out of his clothes after the show and getting into a steamy shower with him. The sound of a cart interrupted her naughty reverie, causing her to jump.

"I didn't mean to startle you," Rose said.

Eden turned her chair around, a silly smile on her face. "It's okay."

"From the look on your face, I gather you were thinking about your hunk of a man."

"You caught me," Eden said.

"You remind me a lot of myself when I was younger."

"And I hope I'm like you later in life."

Eden saw tears form in Rose's eyes.

"Are you okay? I hope I didn't upset you."

"I'm fine. Excuse me," she said and raced out of the office.

Her reaction puzzled Eden, but had to put that aside for now as her meeting would start shortly. Once the entire group arrived, Rose, who had composed herself, wheeled the coffee cart around. When she was done, she exited the room, closing the doors behind her. Eden stood at the head of the table.

"Thank you all for taking time out of your busy schedule. I won't keep you long. I just wanted to let everyone know that I'll be waning down coming into the office daily. I trust Olivia to run things. I do still want to visit each of your areas and learn a bit about what you do, but past that, I will stay a silent owner. I will check in from time to time and will always make myself available should anything arise. Olivia, anything you'd like to add?"

"Thank you, Eden. Nothing."

"Wonderful. Please help yourself to more coffee and treats on your way out. Thank you all for your time this morning. Larry, would you mind staying for a moment?"

"Of course."

Once everyone left the room, Eden closed her office door.

"I need to ask you something personal," Eden said.

"What is it?"

She showed Larry the letter she found, particularly the part about telling her the truth.

"Do you know what he was referring to?"

"I do, but I'm afraid I'm not at liberty to say."

"Why not?"

"There are parties involved that would need to consent prior to any disclosure. I am willing to inquire, but I'm bound by privilege not to reveal it otherwise."

"I understand. Thank you."

"Is there anything else?"

"Do you or HR need to be here when I give Rose her raise?"

"No. We've already prepared the offer letter, and I have signed off on it, so you are good to just present it to her. Shall I send her in?"

"Please."

Larry headed out and let Rose know Eden wished to speak with her.

"Larry said you wished to speak with me."

"Yes. Please have a seat," Eden said, pointing at the chair across from her desk. Once Rose sat, Eden took a folder out of her desk drawer. She handed the sheet of paper to Rose.

"I've been impressed by your performance, both what I've observed and from records my father kept. I don't, however, feel that your pay is appropriate. I've spoken with human resources and I'm pleased to inform you we're increasing your salary by 20%."

Rose's mouth dropped when she saw the compensation sheet. "Am I reading this correctly?"

"You are. This raise is effective immediately."

"Eden, I can't thank you enough."

"It was my pleasure."

"You're very kind. If I'd ever had a daughter, I'd want her to be just like you.

Eden couldn't help but notice a sadness in Rose's eyes when she said that. That sounds just like me, Eden thought to herself.

"That's so nice of you to say."

"I'd better get back to work and earn this extra salary," Rose said, then walked back to her desk.

Eden sat down, her mind swirling from everything that happened today. She couldn't shake the feeling that the answer was right in front of her. She shook her head to clear the fog. She looked around for anything that might point to whatever her father had kept hidden, but to no avail. There was a safe in her father's office, but she didn't know how to access it.

"Larry Paul, may I help you?"

"It's Eden. I need another favor. Can you come up to my office?"

"Of course."

A few minutes after she called him, Larry arrived at her office.

"Do you know how I can open the wall safe?"

"Yes, your father entrusted me with an envelope containing the instructions, to be opened only by his next of kin, so that would be you. I thought that's why you asked me here, so I brought it."

"Do you need to review anything before I open it, given what we discussed earlier?"

"I can't say yes to that, as all contents belong to you. I would encourage some discretion only because I have no knowledge of the contents. To protect yourself, I would suggest you review the contents on site in case there is any information not meant for the public."

"I understand, thank you. If I request you to stay, can you? I would feel more comfortable."

"In that case, yes, since you made the explicit request."

"Thank you. If you don't have time today, I'm fine with waiting."

"I have time."

Eden opened the envelope and removed the instructions. She opened the safe and found a file folder. She just held it and stared at it, afraid of what might be inside. She handed the folder to Larry.

"Can you look inside and just tell me if this is something proprietary that I need to keep onsite, or I can take it home and look at with Johnny?"

"Of course," Larry said as he glanced inside the folder. Eden saw him swallow hard, then hand it back to her. "You're safe to take it home. In fact, I encourage you to wait until then to look."

"Wow, not what I was expecting you to say, but thank you. I think I'm going to head out soon. I appreciate you coming up and helping me with this."

"You're welcome. Once you review the file, please let me know if you need anything."

"I will. Have a good evening."

"You as well," Larry said as he left Eden's office.

Eden grabbed her cell and dialed Johnny's number.

"Hello," she heard his sexy voice say.

"Hi. I'm getting ready to head home. Can we order Chinese and stay in tonight?"

"Of course. Hey, you okay?"

"I don't know yet."

"What's going on?"

"I don't know that either. We'll talk when I get home," Eden said, then disconnected before he could ask her any more questions.

She drove home wracked with guilt about breaking off their call, but she just felt like she needed to be home with him. She put the folder in her bag, locked her office, and headed down to her car. She threw her bag on the backseat so she couldn't reach it on the ride home. Johnny was waiting on the porch for her when she pulled in, a concerned look on his face. He walked over to her car.

"Baby, talk to me. I can tell something is wrong."

"Can we go inside first?"

"Of course. I already ordered the food. Should be here soon."

"Thank you," she said.

Eden headed into the bedroom to change into her jammies. She grabbed the file folder out of her bag and put it on the kitchen table.

"What's that?" Johnny asked.

"I'm not sure. I read the letter after you gave it back to me and there's something that's been nagging at me. In the end, my father alluded to telling me the truth about something. I asked Larry if he knew what it was."

"And did he?"

"Yes, but he couldn't tell me."

"Why not?"

"All he could tell me is that there were other parties involved that would need to give consent."

"I'm confused."

"Believe me, so am I. But, anyway, I saw my father had a safe in the office and so I asked Larry if I could open it. He said I was because I inherited everything, so he gave me the instructions, which my father had sealed and given to him for safekeeping."

"What was in there?"

"Just this folder. I had Larry look at it first to make sure it wasn't something I had to leave on site. He handed it back and encouraged me to wait until I got home to open it, so here we are."

"What do you think's in there?"

"I get a feeling it's what my father wanted to tell me. This day has not at all turned out like I thought."

"Did something else happen?"

"I was chatting with Rose. I told her I hope I'm like her later in life. She teared up and excused herself."

"That's strange."

"I thought so too."

"Are you going to look in the folder?"

"Yes. Here goes."

Johnny watched her jaw drop as she read. She closed the folder and just stared at him for a moment, then took a deep breath.

"Priscilla's not my mother."

"What?"

"My father had one night of indiscretion and nine months later, I was born. To preserve my family's reputation, Priscilla raised you as her own."

"Oh my god, is Rose your mother?"

"Yes. No wonder Priscilla resented me. And now I understand what happened earlier with Rose. What do I do now?"

"I think you need to talk to her, I would recommend away from the office."

Johnny reached out and took Eden's hand, squeezing it for reassurance. He sat there, just holding her hand, until he heard a knock at the door. Johnny answered the door and returned with a bag of food. He put all the cartons out on the table and grabbed two place settings and a bottle of wine. They sat quietly and ate. They were just getting finished cleaning up when they heard another knock at their door.

"I wonder who that could be," Johnny said.

Eden was still in the kitchen when she heard Johnny say, "Hello Rose. Please come in and make yourself at home."

Eden walked out of the living room, as Rose was just sitting down on the couch. Rose looked up when she saw Eden approaching.

"Go talk with her. I'll be in the bedroom," Johnny said.

Eden walked over and sat down next to Rose. Her mother.

"I don't know where to begin," Rose said.

"I don't know what to ask. Tell me what happened, please."

"I had just started working for your father. He was at the office late one night, after another wicked argument with your mother. He told me about what had happened, and he was feeling low about how he let her control him. One thing lead to another."

"But how did I end up being raised by Priscilla?"

"A scandal like that would have damaged your father's reputation, as well as that of the company. Your grandfather would not allow that. I was young and naïve. They convinced me that their money and reputation would allow for you to have a much better life than you would have had with me," Rose said as tears rolled down her cheeks.

"But I didn't. Sure, they had a lot of money, but Priscilla resented me from as far back as I can remember. Now I understand why."

"I can't apologize enough."

"There's no need. You did what you thought was best for me."

"Not that I'm not grateful, but how are you so calm about this?"

"How much do you know about my childhood?"

"Very little. Your father never spoke of you around me until you opened the restaurant."

"Priscilla was very unkind to me. She made sure I knew I was beneath her. I just never knew why. I wasn't allowed downstairs when they had gatherings. I'm so relieved that I'm not hers by blood, that I'm happy to have found out the truth."

"You don't know how relieved I am to hear you say that. I was so sure you would hate me."

"There's no way I could ever hate you, Mom."

"Did you just call me mom?"

Tears streaming down her face, Eden hugged Rose. "I hope that's okay."

"More than okay. So many times, I've wanted to find you and tell you, but I was bound by an NDA. Once your parents passed, I was no longer held by that, but I didn't want to just spring it on you with everything else."

"I'm so glad I know now."

"As am I. You can tell your handsome fella he can come out now," Rose said.

Johnny walked out and stood behind Eden, his hands on her shoulders. "I must admit that I could hear your conversation and I'm so happy. Eden and I have lost a lot of family between us, so for her to find out about you is amazing. I found out I had a twin sister I never knew about, which is why I came here. If not for that, I'd never have met my angel."

"I'm so happy to hear that. I need to ask, Eden, how you want to handle this at the office."

"I think we may want to discuss with Larry how best to proceed. I'll schedule some time to sit down and talk with him."

"Okay. I must go, but before I do, I need to thank you for tonight."

"I'm the one who needs to say thank you."

Rose stood to leave. Eden followed suit and hugged her mother. Rose then hugged Johnny. Johnny walked her to her car as Eden watched from the porch. He walked to the porch and pulled her tight.

"Baby, this is amazing. I know how elated I was when I found out about Hannah after all the people I'd lost. Now, you get to experience that too."

"I'm still a bit in shock, but what I feel most is relief."

"How so?"

"I'm thankful I don't share life's blood with Priscilla. And now I feel like a jerk."

"Why?"

"Your birth mother."

"Baby, don't feel that way. I'm so happy that you got this amazing news."

"I love you."

"I love you, angel."

"Let's go inside and go to bed."

"Tired from the day?"

"No, but I will be if you do a good job," she purred.

"Damn woman."

Chapter Twenty-Three

A month had passed since Eden turned over control of Mitchell Consulting to Olivia. Olivia's keen business sense and fresh perspective brought a renewed life to the company, increasing clientele and revenue by a large margin. Eden was able to step back and become a silent owner as she planned. Max was having similar success at the restaurant. For the first time in as long as she could remember, Eden didn't have to get up for work. She was sitting on the bed watching Johnny get dressed.

"Damn, you look sexy. Are you sure you can't come back to bed?"

"Sorry, Baby. You'll have to control yourself until tonight."

"Damn."

"Any plans today?"

"I think I might do some writing."

"Naughty stuff?"

"Possibly."

"Well, if you need someone to act it out with, I'm your man."

"Mmm, my sexy man. For now, what would you like for breakfast?"

"I know what I want, but that will have to be my dessert tonight. So, for this morning, I would love an omelet."

"Of course."

After they finished breakfast, Johnny gave her a kiss goodbye that left her lightheaded. She grabbed her laptop and sat out on the back patio to work on her first full-length novel. She heard a knock at the door, so she walked around front and saw Lizzie.

"Hey. I'm sitting out back if you'd like to join me," Eden called out.

"On my way," Lizzie said.

Lizzie gave Eden a big hug when she reached the back patio.

"I hear it's been quite a month for you," Lizzie said. "Wow, finding out about your mom."

"It was a shock, but one that I'm glad I got," Eden said.

"Yeah, I'm sure. Hannah told me a little about the woman who raised you."

"She knows what I went through, but look at us now!"

"Badass bitches," Lizzie said.

"Damn right!" Eden said.

"So, what are you working on?"

"I'm nearing completion of the first draft of my debut novel."

"How exciting. If you're looking for someone to read it, I'd love to be the first."

"That would be amazing. You're so talented, I'd love to have your feedback."

"My pleasure. So, are you still happy about the guys forming a band?"

"I'm so excited. Johnny did the right thing and sacrificed his shot the first time around, so I'm happy to see him have a second chance to do what he loves."

"I'm excited too. Andy was so down after his brother having to retire and the other guys turning on him. He's known Dean and Mikael for a while, and Johnny fits right in."

"I challenge anyone to find a more sexy, talented bunch of men!"

"Not possible."

"Could I ask you for a little advice?" Eden said.

"Of course."

"How do I become a good rockstar woman?"

"Trust me, you already are. I see how much you love and support Johnny. Just keep being you."

"Thank you."

"Any time."

They sat and talked a little while longer, and then Lizzie headed home. Eden was so grateful to have met these amazing women. She felt like they were family, not just friends. She went back to writing her book and awaiting her sexy rock star to get home. She went inside when it was getting close to Johnny coming home to get dinner started. More than anything, she was excited to serve him dessert later and show him the dirty little thoughts that ran through her head earlier. She was in the kitchen finishing up when she heard the front door open.

"Honey, I'm home," Johnny said.

He walked into the kitchen and wrapped his arms around her, kissing her neck.

"I missed you, sexy," Eden purred.

"If you hadn't cooked this delicious-smelling dinner, I'd get you naked."

"Mmm, baby."

"Have a seat. The food's almost ready."

"I'm a lucky man. I get to eat dinner, then I get to eat the sexy woman who cooked it."

Eden grinned from ear to ear as she put two plates of food together and poured two glasses of wine. After they ate and cleaned up, she told Johnny to take a seat on the couch until she was ready for him.

"How will I know you're ready?" he asked.

"You'll know."

A few minutes later, Johnny heard bongos coming from their bedroom. His jaw dropped when he walked in and saw his sexy woman standing there wearing nothing but a pair of drums.

"Ummm, holy shit, woman."

"Something you like?"

"Oh yeah. I want you so bad right now."

"Mmmm, then come get some."

Johnny walked to where Eden was standing, removed the bongos, and scooped her up in his arms. He carried her over to the bed and laid her down. He joined her and pulled her close, crushing his lips to hers as he ran his hand over her sexy ass. She reached her hand down and grabbed his already-hard dick, stroking lightly. She felt him growl into her mouth as she stroked him.

Gently pushing her sexy man onto his back, she got on all fours and wrapped her lips around his dick. She ran her tongue up and down his cock as she gazed into his eyes. She watched his sexy chest rise and fall as he growled. Her pussy was throbbing, eager to be wrapped around him. She straddled him, grabbed his dick, and slid it inside her body. He pulled her into a tight embrace as she rode him, meeting her with powerful thrusts.

"My angel, nothing is more incredible than being naked with you, being inside you. Listening to your soft moans is the sweetest song in the world."

"Oh, Johnny, nobody has ever touched me the way you do. Mmmm, so fucking amazing."

She could feel herself reaching the boiling point and increased her pace. She screamed out as waves of magical pleasure overtook her body. She heard a deep growl as Johnny emptied himself inside her. They laid together, a tangled mess of sweaty limbs wrapped around each other, chests heaving, their bodies still tingling with passion. They grabbed a quick shower, then got back in bed.

"What are your plans for tomorrow?" Johnny asked.

"I'd like to finish the first draft of my book so I can send it to Lizzie to read. I was also thinking I'd like to enjoy lunch at the park if I can find a sexy man to join me."

"I will be that man."

"I was hoping for Nikki Sixx, but I guess you'll do," she said.

"Nikki Sixx has nothing on me."

"Oh, is that so? Prove it!"

Johnny spent the rest of the night showing Eden over and over why he was the best. The next morning, after Johnny left for work, Eden went outside to the patio and finished her book, then sent it off to Lizzie to review. She stopped in at her restaurant to grab lunch, then met Johnny at the park. While they were eating, Johnny's cell rang.

"Hello," Johnny said. "One second, let me put you on speaker so Eden can hear, too."

"It's Melissa. I wanted to call and let you know that the owner has accepted your offer on the house. I'd like to schedule your settlement appointment. The owner is looking to complete the sale as soon as possible, as he's being relocated for work. Are you both available this afternoon?"

"It depends on the time, as I'm working," Johnny said.

"Would 3pm be too early?" Melissa asked.

Eden grabbed her cell and sent a text. She got a quick reply and nodded yes to Johnny.

"We'll be there," Johnny said.

"Wonderful. I'll see you at the bank at 3. Congratulations to you both."

"Thank you," Johnny and Eden said in unison.

"I texted Hannah and of course she was fine with you leaving early," Eden said to Johnny when he disconnected.

"Thanks, baby. I can't believe that beautiful house is going to be ours in a few hours."

"I'm so excited. I love that we'll be building a home together. And of course, I can't wait until we fuck in every room."

"You're the best, my angel, though I think I need to call you my sexy devil."

"Well, I'm always horny around you, so that fits."

Johnny pulled her close and kissed her with passion. They came up for air when they heard a couple of loud throat clears.

"Is this all you two do?" Andy said.

"Oh no, we do a LOT more than just kiss," Eden said.

"I'm glad we ran into you," Lizzie said. "I read the first few chapters of your book and damn, girl. You're so talented."

"Wow, really? That means a lot, especially coming from you," Eden said.

"With your permission, I'd like to show it to my editor when I'm finished."

Tears filling her eyes, Eden said, "You'd do that for me?"

"The book is incredible. You have a real future there. And Johnny, you're a very lucky man, with the stuff floating around in your woman's brain."

"That I am," Johnny professed.

"You two seem especially happy," Andy noted.

"We are," Johnny said. "A little while back, we put a bid in on a house and we make settlement this afternoon."

"Congratulations," Lizzie said, hugging them both.

"Ditto that," Andy said.

"We'll have you all over after we've finished moving in," Eden said.

"Sounds fun. You need any help moving, give us a shout," Andy said.

"Thanks, man," Johnny said. "I need to get back, especially since I'm leaving early. I'll be home in time to change for our appointment," he told Eden.

"Okay, see you soon," Eden said, grabbing his ass as he walked away.

"We gotta run, too," Andy said.

"Bye, guys," Eden said.

Lizzie waved and Eden watched them head back to their car. She cleaned up the lunch trash, then walked back to her car. She couldn't believe the feedback she got from Lizzie about the book. She spent the afternoon packing some stuff until Johnny got home. They grabbed a shower, then headed out to their appointment. Everything went well, and they left the meeting, keys in hand.

"Can we stop by the new house on the way home?" Eden asked.

"I was planning on it," Johnny said.

They pulled into the long driveway and went inside, both of them standing there staring.

"I can't believe this is ours," Eden said.

"Me either. I can't believe you're mine."

"Always."

"I can't wait to sleep here," Johnny said.

"I can't wait to get naked here," Eden purred.

"Wait here," Johnny said and ran out to his truck. He returned with two beach towels. "Come with me."

Johnny took her hand and led her into the indoor pool area. He started stripping, so Eden followed suit. They got into the pool and Johnny pulled her close, kissing her hard. She could feel his desire as his tongue explored her mouth. All she could think about was where else she wanted to feel that sexy tongue. He lifted her up and sat her on the edge of the pool.

"Baby, get those legs open. I need to taste that sweet pussy now."

She threw her head back, moaning and writhing as Johnny worked his magic on her. He sure knew how to pleasure a woman. She exploded, her entire body quaking. Johnny helped her back into the water. They swam over to the corner steps in the shallow end and Johnny sat down. Eden climbed onto his lap, taking his rock-hard erection as deep inside her as she could. She bounced up and down on his cock, water splashing around them.

"Fuck, you feel so good inside my pussy," Eden purred.

"So fuckin' hot, my angel."

She felt his chest vibrate from the deep growl he emitted as he emptied himself inside her. They took a short swim around the pool to cool off, then got dressed and headed out. After stopping for some take-out, they went home and spent the rest of the night relaxing together on the couch.

"I still can't believe we're going to be living in that beautiful house," Eden said.

"I can't wait to build a home with you, my angel."

Looking up at Johnny, she said, "I never thought I'd find someone to love me until you came into my life. I love you so much."

"And you showed me how to trust my heart to someone again. Thank you for showing me how to live again."

Johnny pulled her in for a kiss and that was the end of relaxing on the couch as they flew to their bedroom.

Chapter Twenty-Four

Johnny and Eden, with the help of their friends, and Eden's mom and her husband Charlie, spent the next couple of weeks moving into their new home. They were all sitting around the living room, enjoying some pizza and beer, when Johnny stood.

"Thank you all so much for helping us. We're planning on having a party in the next couple of weeks. Do you want to tell them the other news?" he said to Eden.

Eden stood next to him. "We've decided that since we want to keep our wedding small, we're going to get married here."

"We'd like all of you to be in it," Johnny said.

"That includes you, Mom. I want you to walk me down the aisle," Eden said.

Rose couldn't speak, so she got up and give her daughter a big hug. The rest of the group joined in.

"We're going to give you one amazing bachelorette weekend," Hannah announced. "That includes you, Rose."

The women went into the kitchen to talk about flowers, dresses, and all the other things that men don't want to hear about.

"The women won't outdo us. Your bachelor party is going to be off the chain," Mikael said. "Charlie, you better plan on joining us!"

"Oh, you don't want an old guy bringing you down," Charlie said.

"Nonsense, you're coming," Johnny said.

"Now we just need to figure out what," Dean said.

"I love Atlantic City. What better place for us than the Hard Rock," Mikael said.

"I'm in," Andy said.

"Same," Dean said.

"It's settled, then. I'll make the arrangements," Mikael said.

The men all looked towards the kitchen when they heard raucous laughter erupt. Knowing what a dirty-minded group of women were sitting out there, they could only imagine what they were talking about. A little while later, they returned to the living room.

"We decided where we're taking Eden for the bachelorette party," Hannah announced.

"Where?" Mikael asked.

"The Hard Rock in Atlantic City."

The men all started laughing.

"Don't tell me you're doing the same," Alex said.

"Yep, babe," Dean said.

"Fine, we each book a different tower and once we get there, the two groups don't see each other until it's time to come home," Hannah said.

"Agreed," Mikael responded.

"Now, let's all head home and let these two lovebirds pretend they're at the park," Andy said.

Lizzie laughed, but everyone else looked puzzled.

"Every time we go to the park, we run into the lovebirds kissing," Lizzie said.

The rest of the group joined in the laughter. After saying their goodbyes, everyone headed out, leaving Johnny and Eden alone.

"I'm in the mood for a swim," Eden said, and headed into the indoor pool room.

By the time Johnny joined her, he saw his beautiful angel completely naked in the warm water. He stripped off his clothes, his erection a dead giveaway of how hot his woman was. He joined her in the pool and tried to pull her close, but she splashed him and swam away.

"So that's how we're playing, huh?" Johnny said.

He swam over to her and tried to hug her, but again, she slipped away, laughing.

"You're in big trouble if I catch you," he warned.

"I'm not scared of you," she said.

Johnny swam over to her again, but this time, she didn't try to get away. He pulled her close, feeling her naked skin against his.

"Fuck, I want you so bad, woman," Johnny said.

"Oh, Johnny, please take me to bed."

They got out of the pool and wrapped themselves in beach towels. Johnny grabbed Eden and threw her over his shoulder, carrying her off to bed. She grabbed his towel off, exposing his sexy lower half. Her hands found their way to his ass as he carried her. He yelped when he felt teeth connect with his ass.

"My, my, you are a naughty little devil tonight, woman."

He put her down and removed her towel. His eyes scanned his beautiful angel from head to toe.

"I need to taste you, baby."

"Mmmm, please baby, I want your tongue between my legs."

"Get that sweet ass on the bed, woman."

After she laid down, Johnny joined her. He slid his hands under her ass and lifted her hips off the bed. He slid his tongue between her folds, licking her slowly. He loved feeling her writhe at his touch. She tasted so good that he couldn't get enough. He brought her to orgasm after orgasm, each coming quicker than the one before, until she couldn't take it anymore.

"Please fuck me. I want you, baby."

"Damn, woman," Johnny said as he thrust his dick inside her.

They fucked hard and fast until they exploded together. He never tired of reaching that magical place with his angel. They laid together, chests heaving, drenched in sweat, basking in the afterglow of their passion. The next morning, Johnny was at work when Eden came by to visit, the biggest smile on her face.

"Hey, babe, you look especially happy," Johnny said.

"I am. You won't believe what happened. Lizzie's editor called and wants to meet me. She loved the book and only has a few minor suggestions she wanted to review. After that, she's going to show me how to self-publish it."

"Oh, baby, that's amazing. I'm so proud of you," he said as he hugged her tight.

"Ahem, you're supposed to be working," Hannah said.

"Sorry, my fault," Eden said. "I had some good news to share with Mr. Sexy."

"Ugh, he's my brother. I don't wanna hear that," Hannah said. "What's the good news?"

"I'm going to be self-publishing my first book. Lizzie had her editor look it over, and I only need to make a few changes."

"Congratulations," Hannah said.

"Thanks. I can't believe this is really happening. It's always been one of my dreams."

"My angel definitely deserves this," Johnny said.

"I have to run, plus I don't want you getting in trouble with your boss," Eden said with a wink. "I'll see you at home tonight. Bye, Hannah."

Johnny gave her a quick kiss goodbye, and Hannah waved. When Eden was gone, Hannah turned to Johnny.

"Have you decided what you're going to do yet?"

"About?"

"Continuing to work here or just focus on the band?"

"I haven't. Has Mikael?"

"Yes, he wants to focus on the music full time."

"What about the store?"

"We're following in Eden's footsteps and putting Kurt in charge of both, with a staff under him."

"That's great. I'm happy to work for Kurt."

"Nonsense. You can't stay here. The rest of the guys are in, you should do the same. Please, think about it."

"Okay, I'll think about it."

The rest of the day was a blur. By the time he was ready to leave, he had decided, but he wanted Eden to be the first to hear it. He opened the door. The delicious scent of chocolate greeted him. His angel was standing in the kitchen, putting the final touches on a beautiful chocolate cake.

"What's the occasion?" Johnny asked.

Eden took Johnny's hand and walked him to where she had her laptop open. He looked at the screen and saw that her first novel was awaiting approval by one of the largest online retailers. In a few days, she'll be a published author. Johnny picked her up and twirled her around.

"I'm so damn proud of you, baby."

"Thank you so much."

"We need to celebrate. I'm taking you out as soon as it's published."

"Yay! Can't wait."

"I have some news, too," he said.

"Oooh, tell me, baby."

"I decided something," Johnny said.

"What?"

"I'm going to leave the store and make music my full-time gig."

"Oh my god, I'm so happy to hear that."

"Mikael, Dean, and Andy are in as well. Stardust is actually happening."

The End... well, almost!

Epilogue

"I now pronounce you husband and wife. You may kiss the bride."

After sharing a kiss that had everyone in attendance fanning themselves, they turned toward their guests.

"Ladies and gentlemen, it's my pleasure to present, for the first time in public, Mr. And Mrs. Johnny Davidson."

Holding hands, Johnny and Eden danced down the aisle to Eden's favorite guilty-pleasure song, Boogie Wonderland, by Earth, Wind, and Fire. Mikael & Hannah, Dean & Alex, and Andy & Lizzie followed them. The rest of the guests whistled and clapped as they danced out. While their guests enjoyed a variety of delicious treats, the wedding party headed off for photos, then rejoined the party in time for dinner.

The following morning, the newlyweds took a private jet to Hawkins Island in Bermuda. For one long, glorious month, they had the 25-acre private island to themselves. They spent most of the trip naked. Eden snapped a photo of each place they fucked, to the amusement of their friends, when they got home.

Andy's brother Alex, now going by Xander, flew out from LA with his wife, Kelly. He agreed to produce a demo album for Stardust. Each morning, the guys would all head to Dean's studio and work on recording, working pretty late into the evening. One night, a few months into the project, the guys asked the women to head to the studio. When they all walked in, the men were beaming.

"Ladies," Xander said, "it gives me great pleasure to tell you that your men did it! The album is done."

The women all ran up and hugged their sexy rock stars.

"When do we get to hear it?" Eden asked.

"We're ready for you to hear it now. Then we are going to debut it at the club," Xander said.

Xander started the recording as each of the couples sat down to listen. The album was amazing, but of course, Eden focused on the drums. She kept picturing Johnny shirtless and sweaty up on stage. When they finished listening, Xander made another announcement.

"We're looking into planning an East Coast tour with another local band, Resurrection. Now, how abut we go out and celebrate?"

The group went down to the club to celebrate. The band they would tour with, Resurrection, was performing that night, so it gave them a chance to see who their tour partners would be. Resurrection included singer Joey Adams, guitarist Jesse Thompson, bassist Nick Peters, and drummer Spyder. Eden couldn't help but think they would make a great rock star romance series. Eden walked up to the bar to grab another pitcher of beer for their table. She heard Joey announce they were taking a brief intermission. Joey walked over to the bar.

"Hey, cutie, how 'bout a beer?" Joey said to the bartender.

"The name's Cassie, not cutie. You can wait your damn turn."

Joey walked back toward the stage with a smug look on his face.

"Sorry, I tire of these ego-maniacs thinking they can order me around," Cassie said.

"I get it. Glad they aren't all like that," Eden said.

"All the ones I've ever known are."

Johnny walked over to the bar.

"I came to see if you needed a hand, my angel," Johnny said.

"Thanks. The pitcher is ours, so if you could take that back to the table, I'll pay."

"You got it." Johnny grabbed the pitcher and headed back to the table.

"He's a musician? Wow, there are some good ones," Cassie said.

"Sounds like you've had an unpleasant experience."

"It was a long time ago, but I will never trust another one."

"Sounds like a good book idea. Readers love enemies to lovers."

"You a writer?" Cassie asked.

"I just published my first. My name's Eden."

Cassie bent down and grabbed her purse. "Is this your book?"

Eden smiled, seeing Cassie holding a paperback copy of her novel.

"Yes it is. Thank you for buying it."

"I love it. Would you be willing to sign it?"

"Of course."

Johnny smiled when he saw Eden sign the book before returning to the table. She sat down just as Resurrection was getting back up on stage. After they performed their last song, they headed off to the backstage area. A few minutes later, Xander got a text inviting Stardust to the dressing room. They spent the next couple of hours getting to know their tour mates, drinking and shooting the shit.

Eden was paying close attention to the band. Joey had that swagger you would expect from a frontman. He was good-looking, and he knew it. Thinking back to when he came up to the bar and being put in his place, she started planning an "enemies to lovers" story between him and Cassie. She planned on doing some digging on the other three guys during the tour.

The following Saturday, it was Stardust's turn to perform. fans packed the place for their album release party. The women had a VIP table down front. Eden sat there, napkin in her hand for the drool, watching her sexy, shirtless husband pounding the skins. Later, he'll be pounding my skin, she thought to herself, then wiped her chin.

Lizzie leaned over and whispered, "You want to lick that sweat off him, don't you?"

"Oh hell yes. He's so damn sexy," Eden said.

"Hey, that's my brother you're talking about," Hannah said.

After not hearing a peep from Alex, they looked over and saw her, head in her hands, staring at Dean. The other girls started giggling, finally getting her attention.

"We get it, girl," Lizzie said.

"It's that look, that voice, that everything," Alex swooned.

The crowd at the club was very receptive to the new music, and the album sold quite a few copies that night. Ticket sales were also going well for the tour, with fans of both bands showing their support. It seemed like no time at all before it was time to leave for the tour. The women were lucky enough to join their husbands, helping with running the merchandise table and anything else their sexy men needed. Every show ended up being sold out and not one crowd was disappointed. Eden could keep up with her writing during downtimes and she had plenty of observations about the guys from Resurrection. When they got home from the tour, Eden told Johnny about her plans.

"I've decided I'm going to write a romance series about your tour partners. I'm calling it The Resurrection Quadrilogy," Eden announced.

"Sounds like a must-read to me, baby," Johnny said. "Let's go get you some material for your sex scenes."

THE END

About the Author

Samantha Michaels was born in 1973 in the small town of Abington, PA and was raised and still lives in Hatboro, PA (both suburbs of Philadelphia). She is married to her high school sweetheart and they have a rescue dog, a beautiful Black Lab named Holly.

When she's not writing or working at her full-time job, she enjoys watching her Philly sports team (hopefully) win, listening to heavy metal/hard rock music, reading, and spending time with friends and family.

Her love of reading began at a young age, thanks to her mother and Sesame Street. Her mom read to her constantly, and by three years old, she was reading on her own, and hasn't stopped. This eventually turned into a love of writing. She was writing for herself and then for a small group of friends, one of whom told her she should be writing books. She took her friends advice and has since published several romance books with plenty more on the way.

Also by Samantha Michaels

The Rockstar Quadrilogy:

Book One: Leather and Lace

Book Two: A Second Shot at Love

Book Three: Pet Shop Passion

Book Four: Silent Angel

The Melody of the Seasons:

Book One: Rockin' Spring

Book Two: Rockin' Summer (June 2022)

Rockin' Autumn (September 2022)

Rockin' Winter (December 2022)

The Resurrection Series...Coming in 2023

Book One: Hate Song

Book Two: Soul to Soul

Book Three: The Highest Bidder

Book Four: Web of Lies

Silent Angel Playlist

Hotel California - The Eagles
Eternal Prisoner - Axel Rudi Pell
Closer - Nine Inch Nails
What Love Can Be - Kingdom Come
Too Late for Love - Def Leppard
Get It On - Kingdom Come
Alone - Heart
Perfect O - Kingdom Come
Still Loving You - Scorpions
Stayin' Alive - The Bee Gees
All I Want All I Need - Whitesnake
Boogie Wonderland - Earth, Wind, and Fire

www.ingramcontent.com/pod-product-compliance
Lightning Source LLC
LaVergne TN
LVHW090935080826
845145LV00003B/756

* 9 7 8 1 7 3 7 2 5 5 8 9 5 *